JUST
JONATHAN

JUST JONATHAN

DONNA SCUVOTTI

To my family:

My husband, Tony
*Thank you for your unconditional love. I'm glad
we get to do this life together. I love you.*

My Dad & Mom
*I am who I am today because of your unwavering
love and guidance. Dad, I hope you find the fluffiest cloud in
heaven to curl up on when you read my book. Your encouragement
gave me the strength to follow my dreams.*

Jason & Ali
*My two phenomenal children. You are my best and biggest
accomplishment. My love for you is beyond measure.*

CONTENTS

CONTENTS

ACKNOWLEDGMENTS

A huge thanks to all the support I've had to make my dream come true.

To Courtney Palomar, you were there from the first sentence. You never once complained, as I sent you endless screenshots of my writing in the raw. Your encouragement kept me going and made me feel like I was really onto something. Thank you for always being there for me.

A special shout out goes to my forever bestie, Lisa Hagins. You were my motivation throughout my writing journey. Your insightful suggestions made me dig deep and allowed me to expand the story, even beyond my expectations. The best compliment was when you told me, you could hardly wait till the movie came out!!! Thanks mate.

To Ali Kent, my favorite and only daughter, you always gave much needed tactful criticism. I knew I could always count on you to tell me the brutal truth and not sugar coat anything. I appreciate this so much because this allowed me to think outside of the box and write beyond my wildest dreams.

Micki Bruner, thank you for being my cheerleader. You gave me great feedback that allowed me to expand on storylines including addiction.

Thanks to Dr. Melissa Ko. You deserve a medal because you endured my constant rambling, appointment after appointment and never once told me to shut my trap. Instead you encouraged me to go after my dream and make it a reality. I'm sure you had an ulterior motive since my writing caused me to need those repeated adjustments. Ha,ha!!!

To my poor husband, Tony. I know you got sooooo tired of me talking nonstop about Jonathan. Not only did I live and breathe it, but you did too, through osmosis if nothing else! I know it took everything you had to not roll your eyes when I talked to complete strangers about Jonathan. I love you for always encouraging me, when I doubted myself and allowing me to follow my dream no matter what.

To Julian and Maisie, my two incredible grandchildren that give me inspiration everyday by just gracing me with their presence. I love you both, more than life itself.

Much thanks to the 1006 Design team. You made this process as painless as possible. I escpecially appreciate Ronda Rawlins for answering my dumb questions without making me feel like an idiot and always giving me a pep talk when feelings of doubt would rear it's ugly head.

ACKNOWLEDGMENTS

Thank you from the bottom of my heart to all of you, my readers. I hope you have loved reading Just Jonathan as much as I loved writing it. This is just the beginning of our journey together.

And last but not least, a huge thanks to my imagination. Who knew you were in there just waiting to come out!!

CHAPTER 1

JONATHAN

I was out past curfew and wandering aimlessly through the forest when I heard it. It froze me in my tracks . . . a blood-curdling scream. It pierced through me like a knife through a piece of paper. Wait. Did I hear it again? Or was I imagining it? I was so distraught at this point that I couldn't be sure anymore. All I really knew was I needed to get home—and fast—but my feet felt like cement, and I couldn't move or even remember where to go. *Think, Jonathan, think*, I told myself. *Get a grip.*

This was no ordinary scream, but, then again, I was no ordinary boy. The scream was the kind that made the hair on the back of your neck stand up, crap your pants, and barf all at the same time. The kind that had terror magnified by infinity mixed with death. The kind that would haunt anyone in their dreams for many years to come.

The forest was dense, damp, dark and cold—always, always cold, no matter the temperature on the outside. The pungent smell of the earth reminded me of camping in the mountains with my family after an unexpected summer thunderstorm chased us back inside our tent. Now, it was pitch black and impossible to see my own hand, let alone try to follow the scream. I stood there, unable to move, shivering and petrified, wanting my mother to come save the day, like she had so many times before, when she was still alive. Oh, my gosh—how I missed her! She always smelled like what I imagined heaven would smell like . . . a hint of lavender mixed with sugar cookies—fresh-baked ones that were soft and warm and delicious. I even loved the ones that got a little crispy around the edges and burnt on the bottom, because they were baked with love . . . a mother's love. My mother's love.

CHAPTER 2

JONATHAN

It happened about a year ago. Well, to be honest, it was thirteen months, four days, and five hours ago—or 9437 hours—but it seemed just like yesterday. Any way you approach it, it was the worst, most horrific day of my life. I escape often to that night, especially when I'm scared, lonely or melancholy. Remembering every single detail, reliving every single second until *it* happened.

The chain of events of that day would change my life forever and rip my family apart. My innocent, loving, perfect little family.

It was fall, my favorite time of the year. The air was crisp and clean, with a slight hint of fire that more times than not elicited a memory of sitting around a campfire with my family, telling jokes and making s'mores. The leaves on the trees were turning vibrant colors—bright oranges, yellows and reds. At home, with a fire burning in the fireplace, my Mom, Dad, and I sat many nights playing charades or just quietly enjoying each other's company. I am an only child. Oftentimes, I wished I had a brother to play catch or share bedtime secrets with, but then I would have to share her—my Mom, the most important person in my life.

On that dreaded night, my Mom had just picked me up from soccer practice. Soccer was my favorite sport, and I was good. Really good. At least that's what I was told. My Mom had said so, after all, and she never told a lie. The coach bragged about my "bionic leg." I always thought that was funny because I really don't have a bionic leg. I'm just Jonathan. Well, anyway, I loved the compliments. They made me feel special and made my head swell a little with pride. My Mom used to call me her "perfect perfect." I'm not sure if that made sense to anyone but me, but it made me feel all warm inside, just like when I ate one of her cookies fresh out of the oven.

My Mom and I were singing our favorite Broadway musical show tune, "The Lion King," slightly off key but loud and enthusiastically . . . about the circle of life and what it meant to be a family. The lyrics always spoke directly to my heart and brought me feelings of contentment.

I was watching the sky turn shades of orange and purple. The sky made the most magnificent backdrop to the colors

of the trees, along with the beautifully manicured deep-bur-
gundy-red blooming oleanders that stretched along the center
divider. I felt warm, happy, loved, and just about perfect. As
perfect as one could feel anyway, because, in all honesty, no
one was perfect—especially all of the time.

And then it happened. A car was coming straight at us
through the beautiful oleanders I had just admired. It was
one of those moments when time stood still and your life
flashed before your eyes.

Crash!!!!

In the blink of an eye, my Mom was gone. Just like that,
my world changed forever. I wish we had been singing a different song, because, to me, now it feels like a foreshadowing
of what was to come. Either way, nothing can change what
happened that dreadful night. Now I would never again feel
her strong arms hold me or smell her sweet breath on my
forehead as she whispered how much she loved me. I would
never again see her beautiful smile.

Why was life so unfair? One minute, you're belting out
show tunes, enjoying the beauty of nature—and the next,
you're gone? Why is it fair that, after a car accident, some
people live on, unscathed, minus the broken heart, and one
unfortunate person doesn't? Or that one person can get behind
the wheel of a car drunk as a skunk, not even giving a passing
thought to the repercussions that might take place? You see,
the night my Mom was taken from me, she was killed by
a drunk driver. I've been working hard to forgive him, but

it's hard not to wish bad things on him. How is it fair that he lives and not my Mom? But then I hear my Mom say, "Jonathan, we must love everyone."

I'm trying Mom, but I really miss you and need you, now more than ever.

CHAPTER 3

JONATHAN

ocus, Jonathan, focus! My mind wanders a lot these days. Especially when I don't want to face reality. Which, if I were being honest, is most of the time. It's painful. Too painful. If I could, I would lock myself in my room and let the walls soothe my soul. Maybe then, I might be able to heal. My room is my sanctuary; I decorated it myself. My Mom told me that I could paint it any color I wanted, because it should be an expression of myself. I took this project quite seriously and finally decided I wanted to represent things that made me happy and alive inside. I painted one wall gold for sunlight, because the sun made me feel warm, like I was wrapped in a soft towel right out of the dryer.

Since soccer was my favorite sport, another wall became green, to represent the fields that I loved running up and down, hearing people cheer me on as I used my bionic leg to score goal after goal.

I had to have a blue wall, because the sky was blue, and beyond that was heaven, where my grandparents now lived pain free. I miss them, too. A lot. I miss the times when they let me spend the night and I got to pick what I wanted for dinner, like it was my birthday, but it wasn't. I was being celebrated just for being me. Just Jonathan.

But most of all, I miss my Mom. I know she's in heaven now, looking down on me, giving me guidance and support and sending me hugs and kisses. Too bad I can't feel them for real, but I know she comes to visit, because, out of nowhere, I get all warm and tingly inside.

The last wall was the most difficult, but I decided on red. For no other reason but that the four colors all together reminded me of a rainbow. Rainbows made me happy and spoke directly to my heart and soul, bringing the promise that the troubles of today would surely pass and bring fresh beginnings.

I was told by most everyone that I was an old soul, wiser than most even beyond my thirteen years. But, lately, I was feeling much younger, just wanting my Mom to envelop me in warm, secure hugs and make me a promise that everything would be all right. In my mind, I knew this was a reality that was not to be, but my heart felt differently.

CHAPTER 3 ... JONATHAN

If only it were that simple—being a rainbow and bringing fresh beginnings. I wished and prayed that life could be different after my Mom flew to heaven. Who was I kidding? I wish with all my heart that the whole nightmare had never happened. But the fact remains that it did. I've been told *a lot* lately not to live in the past and learn to accept reality, but I'm still trying to figure out how to do that 9437 hours later. I think what haunts me the most about that night and losing my Mom is, *Why her?* She was as near to perfection as anyone could be. Have you ever met one of those people that, after you meet them, you can't stop thinking about them because they have an angelic aura? An aura that exudes warmth and friendliness. After one encounter, they seem like your best friend, and you end up telling them all your deepest, darkest secrets you haven't dared share with another soul. My Mom had that unique ability, and countless people, men and women alike, told me at her wake how they felt that instant connection with her. I feel bad for them that they lost a friend and confidante—but not as bad I feel for myself. To me, she was so much more than that.

My Mom was smart. Really, really smart. Not just book smart but common-sense smart, which means a lot more in the real world. I was positive she could have been a brain surgeon or even the president of the United States, but, instead, she chose to be my Mom. And not for one second did she ever regret that decision. That's what she told me anyway, and I believed her. She was also beautiful, with a dimple in the corner of her mouth when she smiled but also one—that looked like a butt—on her chin. She had beautiful, wavy, long blond hair that flowed in the breeze. And her blue eyes were so mesmerizing that, when you looked into them, you could see honesty, love and a fierce spirit to protect those she loved. She used to tell me that, when she was a little girl, she'd always dreamed of being a mother and having a big family. But, after my parents got married, it wasn't as simple as just hoping, wishing and dreaming. Some things just aren't meant to be. They were married ten years before they had me, and only because of IVF were they able to make their family a reality. That and the grace of God. So that is why I am an only child. And why I was the apple of my mother's eye. Oftentimes, when I was supposed to be asleep, I would hear my Dad tell my Mom that she was suffocating me and babied me too much. I never felt suffocated. I could breathe just fine; especially that sweet lavender scent. My Mom and I had a nighttime ritual after my shower to wash off what she called "boy stuff"—snips and snails and puppy-dog tails; she would tuck me in, tell me stories about when she was little, and rub my legs. My legs hurt a lot; she said they hurt because I was growing like a weed. I thought that was funny. She always made me laugh at the silliest things. Right before she turned off my light, she would kiss my cheek, *boop* me on the nose and tell me she loved me more than anything in the whole world. I would go to sleep warm and content and have the best dreams.

Not anymore. My sleep is filled with nightmares now. Most nights, I lie awake until dawn, trying my hardest not to fall asleep, so that I'm not haunted by the night everything changed.

CHAPTER 4

JONATHAN

My Dad is a complicated man. When he was younger, he played soccer, just like me. He would often tell me stories of how he was a star who led his team to lots of victories, and, in our house, he still had the trophies to prove it. I wanted to be just like him, before he changed. It made me so proud when he would run up and down the sidelines at my soccer games cheering me on and giving me the confidence I needed. He was proud of me, and that made me have one of those head-swelling moments.

He is as handsome as my Mom was pretty. He is the tall, silent type who got all awkward in social settings but was funny and talkative at home with me and my Mom. I was so much like him. I didn't have any friends because I was so quiet. That made for some lonely times for me. Especially after my Mom died because I had nobody to talk to. Nobody to share my crippling grief with. So I withdrew. Farther and farther into my shell. Not only had I lost my Mom that night—I lost my Dad, too.

Even though my Dad was still walking, breathing and alive, he was dead inside. He had lost his one true love, and he fell apart. When I needed him the most, he was not there for me or for himself. It was hard watching him struggle to even get up in the morning, but it was harder for me not having anyone to talk to. He went from being the best Dad in the world to not even caring if we had food in the house or wondering where I was. We used to always have a date on Saturday, when it would be just the two of us. It really didn't matter what we did, as long as we were together. We would go to baseball games, ride bikes, fly kites. You name it. It always made my week fly by knowing I had those times to look forward to. But not anymore. He gave up on everything, including me, and, no matter what I did or said, I couldn't get through to him.

I understood why my Dad was handling my Mom's loss so terribly—he'd lost his best friend. His soul mate. His other half. They had grown up living next door to each other, and my grandparents used to joke about how wonderful it would be if someday they got married. They fell in love the first time they laid eyes on each other, and, from that day on, there was just nobody else who interested them. It was kismet or fate or just plain and simple love at first sight. No matter what you called it, it was special. Since they were both only children, they spent countless play dates together. Family vacations at the lake where they both would spend hours swimming and then napping under the shade of the old oak tree. At night, they'd fall asleep under the stars surrounded by fireflies they used as night lights. It was a magical time in their lives that they often talked about—the many summers they spent living for the day and dreaming of the future . . . a future together, surrounded by many children. They talked for hours on end about growing old together and what fun it would be to bring their children to the lake house, where they'd fallen deeper in love every summer. Dreams shattered by just being in the wrong place at the wrong time.

CHAPTER 5

JONATHAN

While I stood on the damp ground in the woods, I strained to get my bearings. I had been wandering lost in thought. Reliving the past, as I so often did. Actually, *all* the time, even though I was often told it wasn't healthy. But how could I not? It defined me now. It was who I was and what I had become. Did I hear voices, or was I hearing things again? That happened a lot, too.

Countless times, I thought I heard my Mom calling me for dinner or telling me she loved me, but it was just my imagination. I wanted it so badly to be true, but this was my fate now. Alone and lonely, not knowing reality from a dream. How had this happened to me? But, more importantly, why?

As I wrestled with this thought, I was startled into reality by a different smell. It wasn't just the crisp, clean smell of damp earth and pine needles but the unmistakable smell of fire, more importantly, a campfire. I knew this smell well because when I had a family, we would camp in the mountains a lot. Those times were so much fun. We spent our days hiking and discovering all that nature had to offer, and, at night, we hung out by a campfire and told scary stories. I remember one time my Dad and I had a farting contest, but nobody won because my Mom made us stop, rambling something about us being gross and disgusting. When we were hiking, we often stumbled upon a freshwater creek, where we would take a dip to clean off the dusty dirt from our hike. It was always so cold at first but so refreshing I didn't mind. I loved seeing the wildlife in their habitat, too. I wasn't scared of being attacked by a bear or mountain lion, because my Dad was always there to protect me—plus I always thought of myself as a modern-day Dr. Doolittle. Animals and I had a mutual understanding, and they all seemed to love me as much as I loved them. I always thought animals had a sixth sense that alerted them to mean people.

Smart that way. Too bad people didn't share that sixth sense with the animal kingdom, because there were some very mean people in the world who just wanted to harm others, and, unfortunately, people were too trusting.

I'd always wanted a dog to share my life and bed with. A dog I could tell my secrets to, go on adventures with, and just snuggle into her fur to feel warm and secure. I could picture her. My best friend. My only friend. She was a golden retriever, and I wanted to name her Canela. It was the Spanish word for "cinnamon," and it's the color I envisioned her fur to be. I had dreamt about her for years and begged my parents relentlessly, but to no avail. I was always given the same answer time and time again. "Your Dad is allergic," my Mom would say. Didn't they have medicine for that? A small price to pay for the undying love of your faithful companion. Oh, how I wish Canela was by my side now. She would know what to do. And where to turn to find our way home. But alas, it was just me, petrified, lost and alone.

First of all, I needed to figure out where I was and how far I had ventured off the path. How far had I gone when I first heard the blood-curdling scream? The scream that started my spiral of deepest, darkest thoughts. The thoughts that were always in the back of my mind but were allowed to come out only at vulnerable times. And I was vulnerable. In a very fragile state, I was told. I often caught small snippets of conversation from well-meaning people about me being on the verge of a nervous breakdown or suicidal. They didn't think I heard, but I did, and I didn't like people talking about me or, even worse, speculating. If they had gone through losing their Mom in front of their own eyes, maybe they could understand. It was hard, and I struggled—but *suicidal*? Nope—not me!

CHAPTER 6

JONATHAN

One rainy Saturday afternoon, my Dad and I were sitting in front of a roaring fire, watching a show about survival. I remember bits and pieces, but, to tell you the truth, I was more interested in how delicious my Mom's special homemade hot chocolate with the teeny-tiny marshmallows tasted than worrying about how to survive in the wild and find your way home when you became lost. Now, more than ever, I needed to conjure up what little knowledge I had retained and form a plan. I knew I needed to find my way out of the thick pine trees that were jabbing me in my face and arms every time I turned, but first I needed to decide if I had the courage to follow the scream and/or investigate the campfire smell. I really had nowhere I needed to be. My Dad couldn't care less where I was or even notice I was gone. I could fall off the ends of the Earth, and he'd probably be relieved I was gone so that he could submerge himself deeper into his depression and let the demons take over, once and for all.

It seemed like an eternity since the scream had penetrated my soul, but, in reality, it had probably been more like half an hour. I listened intently for any other sounds: screams, voices, crunchy leaves under footsteps, but it was so quiet that I could hear my tummy growl. I had forgotten to eat again. Actually, more like there wasn't anything to eat. My Dad couldn't be bothered with such a meaningless task as grocery shopping when he could spend his days closed up in a dark room with a bottle of gin instead. I really couldn't understand why he would want to drink alcohol when that had been the main contributing factor to my Mom's death, but depression and sorrow made you do crazy, uncharacteristic things. So, I tried to understand and have patience in hopes that, if I gave him enough time and space, he would find his way back to being my Dad again. The Dad I loved so much and needed so desperately.

As I put all my thoughts of my Dad and my tummy aside for now, I concentrated on my surroundings. The air now smelled of damp earth, pine needles, and campfire soot. A welcoming smell that conjured up so many memories. Good, happy memories, but I stayed focused this time and really concentrated. I could still make out the smokiness of a fire somewhere in the distance, but I couldn't see any smoke.

The forest was very dense, so it was difficult to even see the sky. I knew that it was pitch black outside, nary a star in sight. That was rare. Recently, I'd spent many nights wishing on stars. Wishing for things that could never be, but it didn't hurt to put out the effort of a good old, heartfelt wish. They never came true, though, because my Mom was still gone.

Speaking of Moms—what would my Mom do if she was faced with my current dilemma? That answer was easy. She would hightail it out of here as fast as her legs could run. I didn't get my sense of adventure from her because she was a scaredy-cat. I, on the other hand, was always up for a good old adventure, especially anything that flirted with danger.

CHAPTER 7

JONATHAN

The forest in the Pacific Northwest of the United States was thick and tall. And breathtakingly beautiful. The trees and mountains are one of the reasons I loved living in a town called Mount Sierra, Oregon. It was a beautiful, quaint little town that I was very proud of. I used to brag about how my great-great-great-great-grandfather used to pan gold by the majestic streams and then founded and named the town after his beloved Labrador Retriever.

Sightseers from all over would line up on Main Street during the summer months to visit the little shops. The shops were mostly locally owned and sold trinkets, souvenirs and the best ice cream ever. When I got older, I wanted to get a job there just so I could eat mint chocolate chip ice cream every day. It got a little crazy in the winter months, too, because we had a ski resort not far away that attracted skiers from near and far. The locals didn't mess with that part of town, though, because we all knew where to go to get away from the hustle and bustle.

The only thing I didn't like about it was that we had to drive to do a lot of stuff. Like my soccer. If we hadn't been in the car that day 9437 hours ago, my Mom would still be alive, and my life would be happy, meaningful and oh-so-very different. I most likely would not be in this predicament, either. I would be curled up warm and content in my rainbow room, dreaming of Canela and soccer instead.

As I put those thoughts behind me, I used my spidey senses to home in on the campfire aroma. It was faint but noticeable, so I knew it was within hiking distance for sure. Now, more than ever, I wish Canela was by my side not only for companionship but protection. Even though I didn't scare easily, I was petrified right now, partially because I was lost, but also because it was pitch-black, and I had heard the most frightening scream known to mankind. A triple whammy in my book.

Trying to maneuver my way around the pine needles to prevent them from poking my eye out but still staying focused on where I was stepping, all the while trying to be extra quiet so I could sneak up on the campfire, proved to be no easy feat. Branches crunched beneath my feet, and I could hear myself breathing heavily. I wasn't sure what I would find, and

I definitely wanted to have the upper hand. As I was walking, I tried to let my nose guide the way, and it didn't fail me. After about fifteen minutes of zigzagging and dodging pine needles and uneven ground, I came to a clearing of sorts. There were still trees, but they were more sparse. The smell was stronger, so I knew I was on the right path.

This is when I started second-guessing my decision. Was it foolish of me to follow the campfire? After all, I was alone and unprepared. I didn't care much for owning guns. They usually did more harm than good, and many accidents happened due to pure carelessness, but I sure wished I was packing one now. You know—just in case. As I continued to dodge around trees, I saw smoke. It wasn't billowing but enough for me to know that the fire was still burning.

When I rounded the corner, I saw him. He was a tall, heavy-set man with unkempt longish hair and a graying beard, wearing a red flannel shirt under a pair of overalls that had holes in the knees and what appeared to be bloodstains. His presence was overpowering, and it made me catch my breath. He hadn't seen me, so, if I wanted to hightail it out of here, it was still an option. An option I was weighing very heavily right now. His head was bent down, looking at something, while his hands hung by his sides. They were huge and callused, and his overall appearance frightened the crap out of me.

CHAPTER 8

JONATHAN

The campfire had been started with pine needles and broken branches inside some rocks that more than likely had been lying around here and there. I didn't see a cabin nearby, but I knew there had to be something close. I realized then that I had been holding my breath as I took in my surroundings, which made me gasp. As I evened out my breathing and evaluated my next step, I moved a bit to try to see what he was so intently staring at. I was hoping that my eyes were not playing tricks on me, because on the ground was a leg. I knew it was a leg—and human—because it still had a black-and-red running shoe attached. The top of the leg above the knee was gnarled, and bone was sticking out at all angles, jagged and sharp. There was a puddle of blood under it that looked fresh.

I freaked out and let out a squeal that caught his attention. He looked around with his beady little eyes, trying to figure out what or who had made that sound. I stood dead still, like my life depended on it, which at this very second I felt was a distinct possibility. He turned and started walking toward me. He had a hitch in his get-along, which gave me the upper hand because I knew that, with his limp, I could outrun him. The only problem now was that I couldn't move. My heartbeat was pounding in my ears, and I couldn't feel my legs. I was frozen, like I was when I had heard the scream. Did the leg belong to the screamer?

I prayed with everything I had for my Mom to give me the strength I needed to run like the wind, and she came through for me! He had made his way over to me and was now an arm's-length away when our eyes locked. I swear, I looked deep into his soul, as he looked at me with utter confusion and a mixture of pain and abandonment. The sadness made me almost feel sorry for him for the split second it took for me to get my footing and run as fast as I've ever run in my life. I thought of it as *my freedom run*. I was terrified that he would come after me. But when I looked behind me, he wasn't there. He hadn't even tried, which confused me even more. He was standing in the same spot where I'm positive I had lost control of my bladder—just a little, and I'd never admit it to anyone, ever. Why had he not come after me if he thought I had seen the spoils from his kill? Why did he look so confused and sad?

As I contemplated this, I continued to dodge and weave my way back to the scream spot.

Once I reached that location, I would be able to find my way home, hopefully. When I was little, my Mom read me fairy tales a lot, and I remember one in particular that was helping me all these years later. I can visualize sitting on my beautiful Mom's lap as she read me "Hansel and Gretel." I also remember feeling so secure and loved. If I was remembering correctly, and I'm pretty sure I was, a brother and sister were lost in the woods and used white pebbles to mark their path home. But once they returned home, they were locked out by their evil stepmother, so then they used breadcrumbs—but birds ate them all. They eventually stumbled upon an old witch, who took them in, only to fatten them up and eat them.

It was a little crazy how much my life was resembling this Brothers Grimm story right now. I was Hansel lost in the forest, and my Dad was the evil stepmother who didn't want me. Now I wondered if the scary man was symbolizing the witch. I hadn't had the foresight to load my pockets full of pebbles, and, since there was no bread in any cupboard at home, I was relying on footprints and broken branches. My plan worked just like magic, and I found the spot easier than I thought. Now that I had arrived here safely without any incidents, I had time to catch my breath, evaluate my situation, and try to decipher what I had just witnessed.

CHAPTER 9

JONATHAN

First things first: I examined myself for trauma to my body. My favorite blue jacket was ripped on the sleeve, and I had various scrapes on my face and hands from the trees, but nothing too deep or alarming. My tennis shoes were covered in dirt and mud that made them a drab-brown color instead of the white they usually were. My hair was a disaster. It was matted with what appeared to be a combination of pine needles mixed with sweat. All in all, I'd say I fared pretty well, all things considered. I would have to think of one humdinger of a story for my Dad if he asked what had happened. But, seriously—that was a big "if," because odds were in my favor that he wouldn't even notice. He didn't notice much these days except when his glass was empty and the gin bottle was dry.

What really had me freaked out was the scary man. Had he killed and chopped someone to pieces, or was he innocent and just stumbled upon something totally gruesome, like I had? That seemed unlikely to me, considering the surprised look on his face when our eyes had locked, in one of the most terrifying moments of my life. I had a feeling I would have many more like that, because I knew myself all too well. I was positive I wouldn't be able to stay out of the forest. Now that I knew something had happened, I would need to investigate. Danger or not.

I conjured up his image in my mind. He looked like a wild man, mesmerized by the leg. I swear I had seen what appeared to be bloodstains on his clothes, but that wasn't proof enough that he was the actual killer. To me, it seemed too coincidental that the screamer and the dead person were two different people. I'm positive they were one and the same. After all, the scream *was* blood curdling, like someone was terrified and scared for their life. The whole idea of this sent chills all the way down my spine and made me break out in a cold sweat.

I had lost track of time, but I knew it was the middle of the night, and I needed to get home and curl up in bed before the sun rose over the breathtakingly beautiful mountains. I used the same method I had used to find my way back to the scream spot—by looking on the ground for footprints and broken branches.

I felt like I had aged five years since I'd left my house earlier in the night. I didn't feel like I was thirteen anymore, after what I had just witnessed. I'm not sure if that would make sense to anyone else, but to me, things you witness age you. At least they aged your soul. I had heard the expression once, "older than their years," or was it "wise beyond their years"? Either way, it explained me to a "t."

After my mom was killed, I found myself taking on the role of the parent in our household, and it forced me to mature very fast. It was so traumatic that it burned the childhood right out of me, which was unfortunate, because now I felt like I couldn't relate to anyone my age. Hence why I didn't have any friends. I had already decided that I wasn't going to tell anyone about what I had seen. Partially because I had no one to tell but mostly because I knew people wouldn't believe me. They would just give me a pathetic look, like I'd lost my mind and was now trying to fabricate stories to avoid my reality. I didn't care. I knew I was sane, and I knew what I had seen and heard were as real as my everyday struggle without my Mom.

CHAPTER 10

JONATHAN

As I rounded the corner onto Ferndale Lane, I saw my house in the middle of the street, welcoming me with open arms. It was a beautiful sight. It was an olive-green Craftsman style that was way too big for just my Dad and myself, but my parents had bought it when they were first married. Back when life was simpler and the dreams of filling it with many children was still a possibility.

It was pitch black, which meant one of two things. Either my Dad wasn't home, or he was passed out, most likely on the sofa. He very rarely went out, so I was pretty sure it was the latter. I climbed the steps and sat down in the rocking chair on our sprawling front porch. Rocking soothed my soul and allowed me to ground myself and put things into perspective. I had logged hours on top of hours rocking in this chair after my Mom died.

While I rocked, I spun a tale of lies I would tell my Dad if he asked. He didn't know that I didn't have any friends anymore, so I would just tell him that I was over at Timothy's house. He used to be my best friend before he moved back to the east coast. My Dad paid so little attention to me these days, he thought Timothy's family still lived around the block. I used to spend a lot of time over there, roughhousing and practicing soccer in his huge backyard. Many evenings I would come home with sweat dripping off of me and looking like an unmade bed, so he would think nothing of it and believe my story, hook, line and sinker.

Now that I had this believable lie formed in my brain, I opened the unlocked door and found my Dad passed out in the hallway. At first, I was scared something had happened to him, but nope—he was just drunk. Again. An empty broken gin bottle was lying next to him, and he smelled like he had thrown up as well. It was not a pretty sight, and I was stumped on how to handle it.

Wasn't *I* the one who was supposed to be taken care of, instead of this scenario? All I could think of was how disappointed my Mom would be in him. The love of her life, best friend, and father to her only child was a despicable drunk who had shirked all his responsibilities and chosen the bottle over his own flesh and blood.

After I made sure my father wouldn't choke on his own barf, I left him there to sleep it off. I was starving, but when

I went into the kitchen, all I could find was an unopened can of tuna, a moldy loaf of bread, and an old, shriveled-up apple in the refrigerator behind some curdled milk. I wasn't a fan of tuna, but it was better than my other feeble choices, so I opened it and made my way upstairs, avoiding the loose step at the bottom of the stairs. I made a mental note that, tomorrow, after going to the store, I would have to call a handyman so nobody got hurt. As I made my way upstairs, the creaking made so much noise that I heard my Dad stir. I held my breath because I really didn't want a confrontation—especially in the state he was in and after the night I had experienced. After what seemed like an hour but in reality was five minutes, all was quiet again. My room was calling my name, and, as I opened my door, I burst into tears.

CHAPTER 11

JONATHAN

I wasn't much of a crier, and I was convinced I would never have any tears left for the rest of my life after I'd cried nonstop for days on top of days over my Mom's death. But here I was, sitting on the side of my bed, uncontrollably sobbing. I looked at my bedside clock that was shaped like Super Mario, and it said 3:22 a.m. I wasn't sure it was possible to feel more drained. I was exhausted not only physically but emotionally and mentally as well.

I figured, since I was already crying, now would be a good time to look at pictures of my Mom and me in the good old days, when we went on our infamous family vacations. Memories that I cherished beyond words now more than ever. Pictures of us smiling ear to ear in front of our tent, camping while the sun set behind us, turning the sky magnificent shades of orange, purple and red. Pictures of me as a baby in my Mom's arms with my Dad gazing lovingly at both of us with so much pride and many more pictures of birthdays from the past thirteen years, along with every holiday. I am so happy I have these memories to look back on and was ever so thankful my Mom was an amateur photographer with a camera always close by to get the perfect shot. I finally had to put the pictures away because my trip down memory lane had left me in quite a state. All this crying had turned my nose into a continuous fountain of snot, but it was still clogged up all at the same time. The human body was confusing. I finally was able to get a grip on myself and sat in silence eating my tuna before I crawled under my fluffy down comforter and fell into a fitful sleep.

I dreamt that I was being chased by the scary man from the forest. He was screaming like a wild banshee, hair flying everywhere with the jagged severed leg grasped in his giant hand. My Dad was watching the whole fiasco unfold from his perch in a tree, laughing uncontrollably while I was trying to move away from the grasp of the man, but my legs were stuck in quicksand. I was frantic when my Mom appeared, flying like an angel, with her manicured hand reaching for me. I grabbed her hand, and, just like that, I was free and flying through the air in her arms. I woke up drenched in sweat, confused, but also happy that I had seen my Mom again.

I lay still, giving my heart a chance to slow down while I tried to analyze my dream. I thought I remembered reading somewhere that, whatever you are thinking about right before you go to sleep is what you dream about. That actually made a lot of sense right now, since the chain of events from my night were ingrained in my mind. It also made total sense that my Mom would come and save me because she had always had my back. I figured my Dad was unhelpful because he basically was non-existent in my life these days and just a joke of a Dad. Whatever the dream meant, it left me freaked, and I couldn't shake the feeling that it was going to come true.

I looked at my bedside table, and Super Mario read 7:08 a.m. The sun was trying to rise in the east, and I heard happy birds chirping in the semi-barren trees outside my bedroom window. As I looked out my window, I saw clouds forming in the sky, which usually meant another dreary rainy day. I closed my eyes to try to fall back asleep and hopefully have happy dreams this time, when there was a very loud crash downstairs that startled me out of my sleepiness.

I threw on some dirty sweats, wrapped a dirtier robe around me, slid my feet into my Uggs and slowly made my way downstairs. I was afraid of what I might find. I made another mental note to do some laundry because my clothes were getting to the point where, any day, they might stand up on their own. I heard the sputter of the heater turning over, and I felt the beginning of some warmth. There was quite a chill in the air, and fall was in full swing now.

CHAPTER 12

JONATHAN

I loved fall. Everything about it. The crisp, cool air, the leaves turning colors on the trees, drinking hot apple cider or hot chocolate by a roaring fire, hayrides, and Halloween. Oh, I almost forgot: picking out my own pumpkin to carve my jack-o'-lantern after frantically trying to find my way out of the corn maze. The corn maze was not my favorite, but I went every year because it was tradition now. My Dad, Mom, and I used to go apple picking every year, too. Apples were best in the fall, and my Dad would chase me down the rows of apple trees as I screamed gleefully, dodging here and there. After we got home, exhausted and content, my Mom would make the most delicious apple pie. The smells of cinnamon and nutmeg would permeate the air, and, to this day, the smell of cinnamon takes me back to those happy times.

Halloween is my favorite holiday. Partially because of the candy—if I was being totally honest, *mostly* because of the candy, but also because I get to be something or somebody other than who I really am. My mom always let me pick out what I wanted to be all by myself. I remember one year, I wanted to be Santa Claus. My Mom wasn't much of a seamstress, but she was bound and determined to make me the best Santa Halloween had ever seen. And she succeeded—it was the best costume ever, clear down to the white beard and big belly. It was quite a hit when I went trick or treating because everyone told me they had never seen Santa on Halloween. I felt special and proud of my Mom for all her efforts.

I have had some epic costumes in the past, and, when I was really little, my Mom and Dad and I would all have a theme to our costumes. One time we were the Scarecrow, Tin Man and Dorothy from the *Wizard of Oz*. I remember that one, because I was the Scarecrow, and every time I walked, I left hay in my wake. Another Halloween I remember vividly was when we dressed up like Winnie the Pooh and friends. Winnie the Pooh had always been my favorite when I was little, and I still love him to this day, although I would never admit that, because anyone my age or older would think that was just silly.

My Mom used to quote Winnie the Pooh to me all the time. It is hard to choose which was my favorite quote, but if I was forced to choose, I would have to say that there were two that stood out. I loved when Pooh said, "If there is a tomorrow when we're not together, there is something you must remember. You are braver than you believe, stronger than you seem, and smarter than you think. But the most important thing is, even when we're apart . . . I'll always be with you." And "If there ever comes a day when we can't be together, keep me in your heart. I'll stay there forever." Since my Mom died, I have recited these two quotes so many times I've lost count. I'm just so happy I have the memory of her telling me these. It's really helped me and has made me realize that she really is in my heart. And my soul. Forever and ever.

CHAPTER 13

JONATHAN

I stumbled into the kitchen to find my Dad looking like death warmed over, hovering over a steaming cup of black coffee. The kitchen table had a broken leg and was lying on its side. The kitchen chairs were all askew, and it smelled bad. Bad, like dried barf mixed with sweat and body odor that one would get only if they hadn't showered in weeks. He hadn't seen me yet, and I contemplated sneaking out. I wasn't big on confrontation, and I was afraid of where this might lead.

Just as I turned on my heel, he caught sight of me and yelled, "What the hell are you looking at?" He had a look of hate and rage that I had never witnessed before, not from him, anyway.

Come to think of it, the only time I had seen a look so vile was in the movies, when someone was about to kill someone else. He moved toward me, and, before I could block his hand, he punched me and connected square in my left eye. It caught me by surprise and totally off guard. I lost my footing, fell backwards into the wall, and hit my head. Now I was seeing stars along with the pain in my eye. I could already tell it was going to be a shiner-and-a-half. And then I cried. I didn't want to cry, but the tears just rolled down my cheeks, out of my control.

My Dad stood over me, staring at me. He stood there for at least five minutes, not saying a word—just looking at me with a blank stare. And then, out of nowhere, a single tear ran down his cheek and landed on my arm. I wanted to reach out to him and pour out my feelings. Tell him how much I missed her, too. How much I missed our perfect little family. How much I missed and needed him, but I was scared of how he would react. So, I just sat there on the kitchen floor, crying, hurt and confused. He turned and walked out of the room without so much as a word.

Not that he was sorry, or "I love you," or even, "I need help"—nothing. Absolutely nothing.

I had things that needed to get done today, since it was pretty apparent that my Dad wasn't in the right frame of mind to deal with reality, let alone menial tasks that had been avoided way too long. My mind was made up that today was the day I would become a man. I would be the one to step up to the plate and make sure life carried on. That's what my Mom would have wanted. And if that's what my Mom would want, then that's what I was going to do, and God help anyone who stood in my way.

As I straightened up the kitchen as best as I could, I made a mental list of things to get at the grocery store. I would have to rob my piggy bank that I had stashed money in from birthdays and chores from years past, but if that's what needed to be done, then so be it. I grabbed some ice out of the freezer to put on my eye and headed upstairs to start my day. After all, I had an awful lot to get accomplished now that I was the man of the house.

On my way down the hall, I heard a noise come out of my Dad's room. The door was closed, so I put my ear up to it and held my breath. He was crying—and not just normal crying, but gut-wrenching sobs that came from deep in his soul. I once again contemplated reaching out, but, knowing my Dad was a proud man, he wouldn't want me knowing what was happening behind closed doors. As I walked away, I heard the shower start. I took this as a good sign. Maybe it was going to be a good day after all.

CHAPTER 14

JONATHAN

What I thought had a lot of promise and potential ended up being a day filled with chores, broken dreams and more heartache. I was so hopeful that my Dad had turned a corner, but once I returned home from the store, he was nowhere to be found. Instead, I found another broken gin bottle and a pile of pictures ripped out of their frames, torn into a million little pieces and set on fire. Memories from our twelve years as a family gone up in flames. Luckily some were semi-intact, so I salvaged what I could, picked them up, held them close to my heart, and sighed.

I sat down in my favorite big fluffy brown armchair, where I used to curl up in my Mom's lap and cried. Again tears ran down my face and stung my eye, which was now puffy and turning colors. How had my life gone from as near to perfection as one could get to utter disaster? I allowed myself some time to dwell on this, but time was wasting, and I needed to kick into action if I was going to salvage whatever little daylight I had left. If I could help it, my Dad was not going to self-destruct. Nor was I going to allow for any more self-pity. I had work to do!

My trip to get groceries was interesting. I was trying to be incognito by donning a baseball cap and shades, but I could still feel people recognizing me and staring. Some looked at me with pity, because they knew my backstory, and others because I looked like a fish out of water. Wandering aisle upon aisle, trying to figure out what to buy, was a challenge, to say the least.

When I was younger, I had gone shopping with my Mom, but being along for the ride was different from trying to piece together staples and meals. I racked my brain trying to visualize my Mom so effortlessly cooking for us, so that I could create a meal just like that for my Dad. Maybe that would give him stability and comfort. Enough to where he would slowly start to find his way back to me. And just maybe, it would help me feel better about myself and heal more.

My Dad and I shared more than I wanted to admit. We were both peas in the same pod, trying to find our way in the world and come to terms with losing the woman we loved more than life itself. We were just going about healing two totally different ways. I tried harder than I had ever tried anything else to understand why, for the love of God, my Dad would drink when that was the sole reason his one true love was dead. But I got no answers, and I was left mystified and confused once again.

After putting away the groceries and throwing a load of clothes in the washing machine, I allowed myself a pat on the back. I was feeling rather accomplished and proud of myself. It had taken me 9448 hours to get here, but it felt good. I was taking control of a dire situation and allowing myself a bit of hope.

I decided to take a little nap before dinner, but as I passed my Dad's room, some unexplained force drew me inside. His bed was unmade, and there were clothes piled on a chair and thrown randomly on the floor. It smelled stale, and I could hardly wait to leave when I spotted a shrine, of sorts, set up on a table in the corner. There were at least fifty pictures in an assortment of frames of my Mom starting as a baby until just before she was killed. Different poses, different scenery, but the same beautiful smiling face staring back at the camera. On the table, mixed among the pictures, was her favorite bottle of perfume. I sprayed some and knew immediately that it was a bad idea. It smelled fresh, crisp and clean with a hint of lavender that I remembered so well. I fell to the ground, flooded with a million-plus memories of the times I'd spent with my Mom, and I was choking on both happy and sad tears at the same time. I wanted and needed to remember her, but smelling her perfume overwhelmed me.

No matter how far I had come and healed, I clearly was not prepared for this.

I tried to find solace in my rainbow room, remembering the days I decided on the colors and helped paint the walls. But even the brightly painted walls added not even an ounce of solace to my funky mood. Maybe it was the season, maybe it was the fact that my Dad was at his tipping point, or maybe it was an accumulation of a number of things, but I was depressed. And sad. Oh, so very, very sad. Right after my Mom was killed, I was told repeatedly that talking about it would help. The only problem with that is, I don't have any friends left. I was never one to have a lot of friends anyway, but the ones I did have either moved away or distanced themselves from me because—let's face it: I was a bit of a Debbie Downer.

CHAPTER 15

JONATHAN

I woke up with a headache, but emotionally, I was feeling much better. A good cry or two or three—I've lost count lately—does a world of good. I now had my game face on, and I was ready to tackle anything life threw at me. I was actually getting pretty good at life's curveballs.

Another pat on the back for me. I washed my face and didn't even recognize the image in the mirror. My eye was painful and swollen, turning bright colors of red, purple and blue. It was the same colors as those pretty sunsets we would sometimes get over the mountaintops. Except this was anything but pretty. I had scrapes on my face and arms that were scabbing over but still raw around the edges. I desperately needed a haircut and an attitude adjustment. Mental note to see where I could find one.

As I passed my Dad's room, his door was still closed, and there was no noise coming from inside. I wasn't sure if I wanted him to be downstairs or not. We needed to talk, but I knew neither one of us would know what to say to each other. I took the let's-hurry-up-and-wait approach to see how to handle the status quo. I guess you could say I got a reprieve of sorts, because, when I made my way into the kitchen, there was no sight of him. His car wasn't in the driveway, and his jacket was off the hook in the mud room. I hoped and prayed with everything that he wasn't drunk and getting behind the wheel, but anything was possible lately.

After the day I'd had, I needed comfort food. I turned on the radio, and "Don't Worry, Be Happy" was playing. I took this as a good omen. I lit a fire to warm up the house and sang along. The words of the song were singing directly to me. Knowing I was not alone and that every life had some trouble made me feel oddly comforted, and it reminded me not to worry and be happy!

Crazy how a cozy fire and singing a happy tune can lift your spirits. I felt invincible at that moment, and it felt really good.

My culinary skills left a lot to be desired, but I had the will, so that had to count for something.

While at the grocery store earlier, I had picked up all the fixings for homemade macaroni and cheese, with squiggly corkscrew pasta and sharp cheddar cheese topped with crunchy sourdough croutons and a side of ratatouille. It was just a fancy French stew of mixed vegetables, and I liked to say it better than eat it, but it was my Dad's favorite meal. At least that's what he always told my Mom, but, come to think of it, he said he loved everything she cooked.

He used to compliment her all the time. Whether it was the way she looked or the way she smelled or whatever she cooked. I loved their love, and it was something I wanted for myself when it was time for me to choose a mate. Because of their love, admiration and respect for one another, I understood why my Dad was down in the dumps. He had lost his will to live without her by his side. Now it was my job to let him know I still loved him and that we could get through the darkest of days together and come out on top stronger than ever.

I discovered cooking was comforting. I lost myself in the recipe, and all my cares and troubles took a back burner. *Hardy-har-har* . . . kitchen humor! I can crack myself up sometimes, and I'm the best at combo words. I think my mind works faster than I can talk, so two words become one. My Mom used to tell me I should write them all down because I could have a book full of funny words that I could sell and become famous. I highly doubted this and was convinced she was just being biased, because, according to her, I could do no wrong. I did like the idea of writing them down, though, because now that I tried to recall them, only one came to mind. I was thinking someone was skinny and thin at the same time and said they were "thinny!" I really don't know why I found this so funny, but I caught myself cracking up at the thought of it. Spending this time in the kitchen proved to be more therapeutic than I could have imagined, and laughing over the silliest of memories was downright cathartic.

CHAPTER 16

JONATHAN

I set the table and even managed to pick a bouquet of fresh violet pansies that were starting to wilt and die on the vine. My Mom had quite the green thumb and would spend hours in her garden, singing to her flowers and vegetables. She was convinced they could hear her and loved to be coddled, but, seriously—who didn't? I was shocked that we still got flowers sprouting among the weeds up to a year after she was gone, but I just figured they refused to die, in her honor. As I arranged the flowers, I could visualize her puttering about, picking weeds and scaring off crows. Whatever it was she did, it worked. She had a magical way of making everything better in her presence.

She won her share of blue ribbons over the years at the state fair. Ah, the state fair. I loved everything about the state fair. From the time of year to the smells that would linger on your clothes long after you got home. The smells of churros and cotton candy mixed with stale grease was heavenly. The rides were cheesy, for the most part, but I still spent my hard-earned money on them. I loved the Ferris wheel and teacups, even though they made me so dizzy every time. I still went back for more, even after I barfed behind the House of Mirrors one year. I would try year after year to win a teddy bear by shooting water into the mouths of rotating ducks, but it wasn't to be. But my favorite part of all were the animals. Animals always brought out the best in me. I would spend hours petting them and watching them play. They were so calming to me. My favorites were the goats, even though one year, before I realized what was happening, one ate my shoelace right out of my tennis shoe.

The meal had turned out fabulous. At least it looked good and smelled fantastic. By the time I finished, it was dark outside, and I was starting to worry about my Dad, but I was convinced he would walk through the door any second. I had no idea where he was and why he had been gone so long, but the longer he was gone, the more I worried. After an hour, I decided to eat alone, while my Dad's food got cold on his plate. I'd had such high hopes that this would be our turning point, but I was left disappointed once again. I scribbled a note to my Dad, left it next to his plate of food, and made my way upstairs. I was exhausted emotionally and physically, so cleaning up could wait till the morning. It had been quite a day, and I needed to try to sleep so I could start fresh tomorrow.

CHAPTER 17

MICHAEL

I couldn't even recognize the man I had become. Just a year ago, if someone were to describe me, they would say I was a devoted family man, full of life, lover of all things outdoors, and quick witted. I always put my family first and worshiped the ground they walked on, so why was I turning my back on my own son? Especially when I could tell he needs me so much!

My name is Michael, and I am an alcoholic. I never thought this is what would define me, but I also never thought I would be a widower. My beautiful wife, Emma, had been taken from me a little over a year ago, and, since that day, my life has been in a downward spiral. I try so hard to keep it together, but she was the love of my life, my other half.

My better half. We were childhood sweethearts, and every memory I have, she's there, smiling that smile that could melt a million hearts with that cute little dimple in the corner of her mouth. If I allowed myself, I could still taste her sweet kisses and feel her arms around me giving me the warmest sensation. My security blanket and soul mate.

I'm ashamed of who I've become, and I don't want Jonathan to see me this way. I've parked myself outside our house and have been watching him occupy himself with household chores and attempting to make dinner. I should be happy and proud that he's trying to keep normalcy in our life, but, instead, it angers me. I guess if I had to be brutally honest with myself, I would say I'm jealous as well because he seems to be able to move on, when I'm moving backwards. Who does that, though—show jealousy and anger toward their own child? Their flesh and blood that they're supposed to be responsible for, protect and love? As usual, I'm drunk, so maybe it's the alcohol clouding my judgment. Or maybe it's just too painful to look him in the eye because he looks just like her. My one and only love.

I have been foolish lately by putting not only myself in harm's way but others as well. I have been driving while intoxicated. I know better but can't get myself to the point where I'm ready to listen to logic. After all, losing my Emma at the hands of a drunk driver, I know, all too well, the devastation this can cause. No good could come out of it, but the thought of turning someone else's life upside down doesn't concern me in the least. The only thing I can think about is drowning my sorrows, and alcohol is the only thing that numbs my brain. With a numb brain, I don't fall down the rabbit hole. I've been down that hole, and it's lonely and devastating.

My life has become a vicious circle, and I feel like I'm living my own *Groundhog Day*. In my rare lucid moments, I can tell right from wrong and can start to form a semblance of a plan. A plan where Jonathan and I can begin to rebuild a life without Emma. The thought of that usually sends me straight back to the bottle. Gin is my drink of choice these days, but it makes me mean. I've never had a mean bone in my body until now. It sickens me that I struck Jonathan today. I don't know what came over me. He was just looking at me, wanting to help, but I saw judgment instead. I want to be a hero in his eyes, not some pathetic loser who lost his job and can't keep his life on track. So, I lashed out the only way I know how these days. How can he forgive me when I don't know how to forgive myself?

I used to be an attorney in a two-man firm with an office set up on Prospect Way. It stood out on the street, partially due to the white picket fence and shingles adorning each window, but mostly because of the giant redwood that got decorated with thousands of lights every Christmas. I was successful, and I loved my work. For as long as I could remember, it was my dream to become a lawyer, so when I became disbarred, it was yet another nail in my coffin. Not that I can blame anyone but myself, but it was still a tough pill to swallow. The occupation I adored and flourished at was taken away after repeated DUIs. The last one being the worst, when I had a blood-alcohol level three times the legal limit of .08. Seems like crashing and totaling your car while being intoxicated is frowned upon by the bar. And to think it all could have been avoided if I'd listened to logic. Logic is not big in my vocabulary these days, and I continue to harm myself and the one person I have left whom I love the most.

Emma and I, with my parents' help, had made many sacrifices just so I could fulfill my dream of going to Harvard Law School. I graduated at the top of my class and had offers from high-powered firms all over the country to become a junior partner, but I loved the Pacific Northwest. We spent hours mapping out our future. We wanted to have a big family, and it was very important that we chose a safe place to raise them. We ultimately decided to return to our roots. There was just something about Mount Sierra, with all its small-town charm, that drew us back. And I never regretted it for a day.

After careful consideration, I decided to practice family law. As a family-law attorney, I dealt with a lot of divorce and child-visitation rights, among other things. The main reason I chose family law was that I wanted to be able to help families, specifically children going through tough times when faced with a divorce. I had minored in psychology for my undergraduate degree and felt like I had the knowledge and aptitude to be a Freudian of sorts. Jonathan always thought he was a reincarnated Dr. Doolittle, and I was Dr. Sigmund Freud. Many a night, I burned the midnight oil, wracking my brain for ways to salvage a marriage or at least ease the pain of those affected. Sadly, even with all my knowledge, I couldn't seem to help myself or Jonathan.

It's not as if I didn't try to stop my behavior. I knew I was on a path to self-destruction, but, no matter what my mind said, my heart said something entirely different. Logically, I knew I should walk my happy ass into the house, straight into Jonathan's room, and apologize. Apologize for being nonexistent in his life for the past thirteen months, for losing my job, and for drinking. The list went on and on and on. So many things to apologize for, but mostly for striking him. I made my son bleed, and I didn't even have the decency to apologize.

I was an over-thinker—one of the things I would change about myself if I could. I never take anything at face value but instead always second-guess the simplest of scenarios for hidden meanings and blind innuendos. I try to convince myself that some things were just as they seem, but I never quite accomplished that. I wouldn't go so far as to say I thought people were out to get me, but ever since Emma had died, I just wasn't me anymore. I felt like people looked at me differently. Mostly with pity, which was wholeheartedly understandable, but also with disgust. And this angered me.

When the anger took over, all I could see was black. I lost all sense of right or wrong and allowed myself to lash out when a couple of deep breaths and some meaningful dialogue could have gotten me out of my funk. It was mostly when I was drinking, which was pretty much all the time now. I never had been much of a drinker before "it" happened, but I found it was the only thing that calmed my thoughts and deadened my emotions. Alcohol made me unrecognizable and—bluntly put—just not a nice person. The worst part was I knew this and still continued down this path, because dealing with reality was far too painful.

As I sat in my car, the gin was wearing off slightly, and the crispness of the air was a slap on my face. This is all I needed to conjure up the courage to address the long-overdue elephant in the room between Jonathan and myself. I dimmed the headlights and pulled into the driveway. I didn't want him to see me, just in case I lost my nerve once I walked through the door. I was so ashamed of my behavior.

Just earlier today, I was in such a state after punching Jonathan in the eye that I did something very foolish. I tore all our family pictures out of their frames, ripped them into pieces, and set them on fire. I was so mad that Emma had left this Earth and that Jonathan looked just like her. He not only looked like her, he acted like her. They both had a gentle spirit and a deep love for animals. The only difference between them was that she was the life of the party and could talk to anyone about anything at any time, and Jonathan was quiet and reserved, like me. It's true what they say about opposites attracting.

The house was warm and smelled equally inviting. In the kitchen, Jonathan had straightened up what I had managed to destroy earlier. On the table was a bouquet of flowers from Emma's garden and a heaping plate of my favorite macaroni and cheese with a side of ratatouille—my favorite meal—that he had prepared for me with his loving hands. After seeing this and remembering what I had done to him earlier made me hate myself even more. The food smelled and looked inviting, but I couldn't make myself take even one bite, because it reminded me of Emma. It brought back many visions of her with her beautiful blonde hair, sweating over the stove just to make me a special meal for no other reason than that she loved me and wanted me to know that she would do anything for my happiness. I can see her standing by the stove, but when I reach out to touch her, she vanishes, and I'm left grabbing at air.

Next to the plate sat a note written in his hand . . .

My dearest Dad,

    I miss you. I need you. I love you. And above everything else . . . I forgive you.

    I miss her, too. Please stop drinking, and find your way back to the way we were, before our life was turned inside out and upside down.

Your son, Jonathan

I don't deserve him. No matter who I used to be, I wasn't that person any longer, and he was better off without me in his life. I was nothing but an alcoholic down on his luck and stuck in a world that was now my reality. And just like that, I had lost my nerve to talk to him and instead went to my room with a fresh bottle of gin to drown my sorrows.

CHAPTER 18

JONATHAN

After three hours of tossing and turning, I finally fell into a fitful sleep. Last thing I remember seeing was 1:25 on my Super Mario clock, and now the sun was rising in the east, barely visible through my dusty blinds. It was 7:12 a.m. and time to start my day. As I rubbed the sleep from my eyes, I was painfully reminded of my shiner. I was hoping yesterday had been a nightmare, but the more coherent I became, the more details of the day emerged. I was all of a sudden reminded of another horrendous dream.

This time, my Dad and I were at a gym, and he was teaching me how to box. We both were outfitted with boxing gloves, but mine were all for show because I was the one getting beaten. Punch after punch. First an uppercut, followed by an extremely painful left jab. I fell to the mat in a puddle of my own blood and sweat while my Dad just stared at me with a sinister smile and began to laugh. It was an evil laugh that came deep from the belly. My Mom was yelling my name, but I couldn't find her. I was frantically searching through my tear-stained, swollen eyes, but she was nowhere. Then miraculously, the man from the forest appeared. He offered his massively big hand to help me up. The rest I couldn't remember, which I was thankful for. I told myself I wasn't even going to waste my time trying to decipher the madness of it and leave it at that. Some things were just better left alone.

The house was quiet as a church mouse, with no sign of my Dad. I listened at his door and heard gentle snores coming from within. I had no idea what time he had finally made it home or where he had been, but at least he was home and alive—in one piece remained to be seen. My eye looked like it was fake makeup for Halloween, and my cheek decided to keep it company and turn ugly shades of purple, blues and yellows, too. I would have to stay away from anyone for a while, which was fine with me. I was quite a sight and didn't know how I would begin to explain what had happened without opening up a can of worms that I might not be able to close.

The house looked the same as I'd left it the night before. My Dad's food was sitting cold and crusted over on his plate. It saddened me that he hadn't even attempted to eat, not even a taste. At least for my sake. I noticed the note I had written had been moved, so hopefully he'd read it and knew how I felt. As I picked it up, I saw a dried-up tear stain in the corner. Was that from him, or had I been crying when I wrote it? It was entirely possible, since it seemed like tears were becoming an everyday occurrence for me.

As I went about my day, tidying up the kitchen and rest of the house, I even managed a load of laundry here and there. I kept getting an eerie feeling that I was being watched, but whenever I turned around, there wasn't anybody there. I chalked it up to lack of sleep and my crazy dreams. This domestic stuff had nothing on me—and to think I was only thirteen. Doing chores reminded me of my Mom and made me appreciate her even more, if that was possible. It made me think of her so much, I even attempted some cookies. They were an utter disaster. I burned every single one, and they came out like hockey pucks. I even set the smoke alarm off, but even with all that racket, it didn't bring my Dad out of his room. I was surprisingly okay with that, because I had extended the olive branch. The ball was now in his court, and I was curious to find out when he would come out to play.

After heating up some leftovers from the night before, I locked up and headed to my room. I was going to make it an early night in hopes that I could finally get some much-needed shut-eye. I couldn't help wishing that I had my golden, Canela, by my side, because I could really use a companion right about now. Especially one of the furry variety, who would just listen, with no judgment, just licks and cuddles. Even though I had decided my Dad needed to make the next move, as I walked by his room, I changed my mind. After all, he was still my Dad, even though I was pretty sure he didn't want to be anymore.

CHAPTER 19

JONATHAN

I stood and listened intently but heard nothing. In fact, it was so quiet I had to go check to see if his car was still in the driveway. I held my breath and knocked softly at first, but when I got no response, I tried the doorknob. It was locked, so I mustered up all the nerve I could and called, "Dad, are you all right?" Nothing. Not a peep. The thought of losing my Dad, too, made me freak out a little bit. No matter what tough act I was putting on, I wasn't nearly as brave and together as I pretended. I still loved him and needed him, no matter how mean and abusive he had become. I knocked louder this time and called out once again with urgency in my voice. At least that's what I was feeling, so I hope it came out that way. "Dad, please answer me if you're in there. I'm worried about you!" I was so not prepared for what happened next; I jumped a foot in the air and peed my pants a little when the door shook on its hinges. He had thrown something hard at it and yelled, "Leave me alone! Can't you get the hint?" I turned and walked to my room but did not cry, which surprised me. Yeah, I got the hint loud and clear. My Dad hates me and wants no part of being a family, but I also knew that I would not give up. My Mom wouldn't want that, and that's what mattered to me the most.

My room was cold and dark. And lonely. I needed to somehow help my Dad find his way, but, honestly, I was stumped on how to go about it. I curled up under my comforter to warm up and think but ended up falling asleep. This time I couldn't remember my dreams, which was a welcome miracle I was thrilled with. When I did wake, Super Mario told me it was 4:17, and I had the strongest urge to go explore in the forest. The house was freezing and eerily quiet. I tiptoed downstairs, making a conscious effort to avoid the creaky step at the bottom of the stairs. I found this somewhat humorous and had to stifle a giggle. Why was I tiptoeing when I could have run down the stairs like a herd of elephants and my Dad wouldn't have concerned himself? I chalked it up to old habits being hard to break. I complimented myself on using my head and loading my pockets with bread, just in case I got lost and had to pull a "Hansel and Gretel" moment. The chill in the air had gone beyond a chill to full-on cold, and I could see my breath.

CHAPTER 19 ... JONATHAN

The humidity in the Pacific Northwest gave the air a moist quality that chilled you to the bone, but I was prepared for this with my Patagonia jacket, gloves and multiple layers of socks under my hiking boots. I wasn't sure what I was looking for or even why I was going on this adventure, but I just felt an indescribable pull to go.

CHAPTER 20

JONATHAN

The forest was about a quarter of a mile from my house, and, as I walked, I tried to convince myself that I wasn't cold, just refreshed. Mind over matter was supposed to work, but it failed me this time, and I was shivering despite my clothing. The past two days seemed like it was someone else's life and not mine. In all actuality, the past thirteen months seemed that way. If it was humanly possible to change something by wishing and praying, my Mom would still be alive, and my life wouldn't have taken a 180-degree turn. If only I lived in a fantasy land, where thinking things made them reality. But once again, the status quo slapped me in the face, and I was forced to think about my predicament at home. Home was supposed to give you feelings of warmth and contentment, but it was quickly becoming the complete opposite, and I still had not one inkling on how to change the ever-present funk that loomed.

Before I knew it, I was at the opening of the forest. It was black as coal and dead still. The unknown was somehow enticing to me, and I threw caution to the wind and reluctantly ventured in. The smell of the damp earth is what I noticed first—that and the quietness. The pine needles stabbed me as I made my way in deeper and closer to the campfire where I had seen the scary man and severed leg. It seemed familiar in an odd way, like I had never left. But at the same time, it surprisingly seemed like it had been forever ago, and I was shocked to realize that it had only been the night before last. So many things had happened, but nothing had really changed. I was still missing my Mom as much as ever, my Dad was still being a jerk, and I still wasn't sure how dealing with both these things, although differently, would change me. I had taken a vow to myself of becoming the man of the house very seriously and was committed to stepping up. I just wasn't sure if that would be enough.

I stopped to listen and focus on where I was. I saw broken branches here and there, where I had frantically run from the scary man. I heard two owls in the distance hooting back and forth like they were having a real conversation—either that or taking turns singing a song. Besides my own breathing and the occasional varmint scurrying up a tree, that was the only sound. It was nerve wracking and peaceful all at the same time. I enjoyed the quietness because it allowed me to lose myself in my thoughts and escape the chaos at home, but it also caused me a little anxiety because I wasn't sure what I was about to stumble upon. My sense of adventure won out, as usual, and I inched my way in further and further.

My ears and nose were on high alert, so much so that I immediately noticed a different smell. It wasn't damp earth, pine needles, or campfire but some weird, different smell, like metal. I couldn't quite place it, but it reminded me of the garage when my Dad used to mess around with his circular saw. A while ago, he got a wild hair and thought it would be a fun hobby to make stuff. I would sit out in the garage for hours, watching him construct planters, various animals and a windmill we put in our front yard. One time when he got really inspired, he made a bistro table and chairs for the patio. He was pretty crafty, and I was his biggest fan. Unfortunately, this is one of the many things, me included, he lost interest in after my Mom died.

I tried my hardest to follow the smell, but no matter which direction I walked, it didn't get stronger. It was just a metallic smell that lingered in the air—like someone had pounded rusty nails into every tree. This made not one ounce of sense to me, leaving me baffled and with my mind in overdrive again. Winding and weaving, I found myself right in front of where the campfire had been. It was extinguished, with not a burning ember in sight. I looked around to see if there was anything out of the ordinary I might find. Last time I was here, I had been scared half out of my mind, so being here now gave me an opportunity to investigate thoroughly. If I didn't know any better, I'd have thought I was looking at a normal firepit, but I did know better. And remembering what I'd witnessed last time caused a shiver down my spine. I moved rocks around with my foot and felt confident that I was deep enough into the forest that I could use my flashlight without drawing attention to myself. As I reached into my pocket, I felt the bread I had brought. What a dummy I was. I'd completely forgotten to leave my trail of crumbs, just in case I lost my way again.

My hair stood up on the back of my neck as I remembered the gnarly severed leg. I thought, *I must be crazy being out here by myself.* I could see the headlines now: "Freshman from Mountain View High Found Decapitated and Dismembered in the Forest!" My sense of adventure was starting to wane when I spotted something that took my mind off my fear. The beam of light from my flashlight caught a glimmer in the dirt. It was shiny and round. As I reached down, I grabbed a handful of dirt and what appeared to be a woman's ring. It was a gold band with an inscription inside that read, "All my love, Chris." To say I was excited with a tinge of freak-out would be an understatement. Had this been left here as a clue from the person whose leg I saw? My mind was racing a zillion miles an hour, and my heart was beating just as fast when I felt something wet on my face.

CHAPTER 21

JONATHAN

I turned, startled to see a dog staring at me. Not just any old dog, though, a golden retriever. Just like my Canela. It was excited and started jumping on me, wanting to play. As excited as I was that there was a real live dog in front of me, I was stumped as to where it had come from. I forgot about why I was here and buried my face in the dog's fur. It felt like heaven. Everything I had ever dreamt it would smell and feel like. As I stood up, the dog grabbed my arm ever so gently and started leading me away from the firepit. I had often read how intuitive dogs were, and, when faced with danger, they would seek help, so I followed it. We walked for about 20 minutes in and out of large pine trees when we came to a clearing of sorts. Now that I was out of the forest, it was no longer pitch black, and the sun was trying to make an appearance. The sky was slowly turning a gorgeous grayish-orange hue. In the distance, I could see a big log cabin with smoke billowing out of a chimney perched in the middle of the roof. As we grew closer to the cabin, the dog took off in a full sprint and left me in its dust. Now I was faced with yet another dilemma. Just as I had made up my mind to head back into the forest and continue my mission, the scary man came out of the door and yelled, "Sydney, come here, girl. What have you been up to this time?" The dog ran to meet her owner and commenced to having a full-on lick fest. She obviously was overjoyed to see her owner, and it looked like feelings were mutual. I also had read that dogs were a very good judge of character and would intuitively shy away from bad people. This clearly was not the case here. You'd have to be blind not to see the mutual love and bond between these two. The man looked up and saw me staring, dumbfounded and at a total loss for words.

It's as if time stood still as I contemplated what to do. Fear was getting the best of me, and I was starting to shake seeing him again. Do I run like the wind before he comes after me and I become his next victim, or do I stand my ground and see where that takes me? I was torn. I was on a high after finding the ring and wanted desperately to do some more investigating, but, on the other hand, something was telling me to hang around. I had already decided school wasn't in the cards for me today, no matter what decision I made.

I wasn't in any mood to explain my appearance and figured wearing sunglasses in class would just draw more unwanted attention. So I started slowly walking unsteadily and unsurely toward the scary man. Was I crazy or just lonely? I so wanted someone to talk to—but at what expense?

At the last second, I changed my mind and took off at a full sprint back toward the forest, sweating profusely despite the chill of the morning. I could hear the scary man yelling, "Stop, son! Please don't be scared of me. Come back." I turned to see him standing with his arms in the air and the golden by his side, but I continued to run further and further into the forest, just in case he was like the witch from "Hansel and Gretel." I was in a vulnerable state and didn't need to be lured into a trap.

CHAPTER 22

JONATHAN

Even though the sun was rising, the forest remained pitch black. It felt like the temperature had dropped 20 degrees, and I shivered as I pulled my jacket tight around me. Note to self . . . wear a beanie next time, because I knew myself and was 100% positive there *would be* a next time. Lots of next times, because I was quickly becoming addicted to the danger and intrigue. Not only did it satisfy my hunger for adventure, but it occupied my time and left me feeling accomplished. Somehow, I couldn't help but think I was onto something, something big, and if I could help someone, I was up for the challenge. There was just something about the smell, the coolness and the unknown that the forest offered that excited me.

With my flashlight in hand, I moved closer to where the campfire had been. The smell of metal permeated the air again. It reminded me not only of rusty nails but pennies, but why would anyone bring money to the forest—or for that matter, nails? Out of nowhere, I had a flashback of sitting in my biology class and hearing my professor lecture on the human body. He explained how your body was 60% water and roughly 7% of your body weight was blood. The lecture continued as he explained why blood smells like iron. Holy crap, I had just stumbled upon something major. I had to slow my breathing because I was starting to hyperventilate. The scream, the smell, the severed leg and now the ring. I knew in my soul that they were all connected and that I needed to find out what had happened without putting myself in harm's way.

My imagination was starting to get the best of me as I frantically dug around the campfire like my life depended on it. The ironic thing was, someone's life could very *well* depend on it. I had never been one to believe in ESP, but I was seeing visions of what had transpired, and it wasn't pretty. Visions of pain, screams and death. It was terrifying, and I felt the strongest urge to unearth the truth and bring justice to this poor soul who'd lost their life at the hands of a maniac.

My hands were covered in soot and turning raw at the tips, but I couldn't stop. Not yet. Not until I found more evidence to give me something to go on. My visions wouldn't hold much weight if I decided to go to the authorities and try to explain myself, although at this point that was very unlikely, anyway.

The spot where the leg had been was discolored and a tad sticky. I bent down to smell the area, and the metallic smell intensified tenfold. Right next to the bloodstain, I noticed something barely sticking out of the ground. As I scooped up a pile of dirt, centered in the middle was a red fingernail, jagged on the ends, as if it had been ripped off in a tussle. The excitement I felt was like no other, and I caught myself holding my breath. As much as I wanted to continue digging, I also knew I needed to head home and do some research on missing persons. I tucked the fingernail in my pocket with the ring and cautiously maneuvered my way through the forest.

I was getting better at finding my way and emerged sweaty and filthy. The sun was trying hard to peek through a sky full of clouds, and I felt a raindrop land on my cheek. I must have looked like something the cat dragged in, so I kept my head down and avoided any eye contact. Luckily for me, most people had already left their homes for school and work, so traffic was almost non-existent. As I entered my house, I noticed nothing had changed, which was OK with me. I didn't have the time or the will to have a confrontation with my Dad. Google was calling my name, and I had some research to do. I made myself a hot chocolate like my Mom used to make, grabbed a banana, and headed upstairs to my room to start my day.

CHAPTER 23

JONATHAN

As I booted up my Mac, I replayed in my head everything that had transpired in the last couple of days. This made me dizzy, so instead I typed "Missing persons in Mount Sierra, OR" into my search engine. For such a small town, more results turned up than expected. Had the killer been on a killing spree in my quaint little town while I was so busy wallowing in my own self-pity? I narrowed down the field by adding the date from last Friday night, but got nothing. Duh, that would have been the night of the scream, and nobody would have been reported missing yet. Once "Saturday September 28, 2019" was entered, an article from the *Pacific Sun Times* came up. I caught myself catching flies with my mouth hanging open, and my heartbeat started to race as I opened up the article. The headline read, "Girl Missing While Jogging in Mount Sierra." Holy crap. I could hardly read, my mind was racing so fast.

The article read . . . "Chris Hopkins, age 32, resident of Mount Sierra, has reported his wife Alexa Hopkins, age 30, also a resident of Mount Sierra, as missing. She was last seen when she left their residence, alone, to go jogging at approximately 6:30 p.m. Friday night, September 27th. Chris reported that she often runs along paths adjoining the forest on the east end of town. She was wearing black jogging pants, a red hooded Cal Berkeley sweatshirt, a black Adidas baseball cap and black-with-red ASICS jogging shoes. She also had earbuds and her cell phone with her. When called, there has been no response, and the calls have repeatedly gone straight to voicemail. Anyone with any information should call the Mount Sierra Sheriff's Department ASAP @ (458) 555–1212. This is an extremely urgent matter."

This pretty much affirmed my suspicions that something very bad had happened and that I was at the wrong place at the wrong time. Now that I had what I considered concrete evidence pertaining to the poor missing girl, was it a crime not to come forward? I spent the better part of the day holed up in my room, researching articles on blood, grizzly murders, missing persons in Mount Sierra, including surrounding areas, and withholding evidence. The internet had a plethora of information that I was more than ready to absorb.

I learned my suspicions about the metallic smell and blood were spot on. I'd have to remember to thank my biology teacher one day—and myself for actually paying attention in class. Surprisingly, there had been a total of twelve women, of various ages, who had been reported missing in Mount Sierra and within a twenty-five-mile radius over the past five years. This disturbed me because I tried to see the good in people, and knowing this made me doubt the good in the world. Or at least in my part of the world, which I imagined was safer than most. I read every article about the missing women, looking for similarities. Two things they all had in common were that they were all alone and were all under the age of forty. I contemplated reaching out to the loved ones they had left behind but decided I had enough on my plate just dealing with the most current situation. I also decided it was best I didn't jump to conclusions. Assumptions often caused more harm than good.

At the last minute, I decided to type in "serial killers." If the same person was responsible for all these women from the past five years, I needed to learn everything I possibly could on what I was up against as well as what made this maniac tick. As I read, I learned more than I cared to know. I was saddened about the poor childhood some serial killers had and how it impacted their overall development. Many of them killed entirely for pure enjoyment and thrived on the actual kill, manifesting fantasies they eventually brought to fruition. It was creepy and hard to comprehend this mentality, so I told myself I would research more later, when I had the time to devote to it.

The last bit of information I learned made me breathe a sigh of relief. I was under no legal obligation to come forward with my circumstantial evidence or any knowledge of foul play. A moral obligation was a different story, but I pretended that I hadn't read that part. I wanted to do the right thing. I truly did, but I was not ready to turn over the ring and fingernail until I had done my due diligence. I cleared out a spot in my nightstand and tucked the ring and fingernail inside a hollow box, along with the articles I had printed out from the newspaper, as well as the research I had done. All in all, I considered my day to be a success so far. My main concern now was hoping my moral compass didn't get the best of me. I wanted to do this on my own. More than that, I *needed* to do this on my own.

CHAPTER 24

JONATHAN

I was surprised to see that the sun had set; my tummy was once again yelling at me to feed it. The house was still quiet and very cold. I turned up the heat and breezed through the living room on my way to the kitchen, when something shiny caught my eye. Sitting in the middle of the room was a brand-new bicycle. Not just any bike, but a Trek mountain bike. The bike I had been asking for as long as I could remember but was always told I needed to wait until I was older and responsible enough to take care of it and not lose it. I couldn't contain my excitement and let out a scream of joy and began jumping up and down. It was red and absolutely the most beautiful thing I had ever seen. As I leaned over to revel in its greatness, I noticed a red ribbon attached to a piece of paper tied around the handlebars. It read "I'm sorry. Dad." I immediately looked around, expecting my Dad to be there with a huge smile and open arms, but I was alone. Mixed emotions flooded over me. "Dad, are you home?" I called. Silence was my answer, and I couldn't help but feel disappointment wash over me. Maybe I was living in a fantasy world, but this act of kindness gave me hope that we had jumped a major hurdle and were headed in the right direction.

I forgot about my hunger and took my bike for a spin, forgetting all sense of right and wrong. Even though it was technically a mountain bike and was meant to be used as such, I didn't care in the least. I was giddy with excitement and took off like a bat out of hell, leaving fallen leaves fluttering in my wake. I must have ridden for an hour, freezing and not even caring. My hands were nearly frozen to the handlebars, but the wind in my face and the joy in my heart made it tolerable. This is just what I needed to lift my spirits, and, by the time I finally made it home, the smile could not be erased from my face . . . until I walked through the door.

My Dad was standing in the entryway with his arms crossed and a sourpuss look across his face. A half-empty gin bottle sat on the entry table next to a double old-fashioned glass full of gin straight with a slice of lime floating on top. I knew the minute I saw his face, his stance and the alcohol that this was not going to be the reunion I had hoped for. I wasn't going to let this get me down, though, and decided to take the high road. I smiled and said, "Dad, thank you so much for the bike. I absolutely love it!" Not waiting for him to say anything nasty to ruin my euphoric mood, I started gushing about how great it rode and how I could hardly wait to ride it to school. My Mom used to drive me, but since she'd been gone, I'd had to walk, and, quite frankly, I was sick of it.

Before any more words could come out, he started yelling nonsense at me to go to my room and that I was grounded for a month for being careless and immature. I stood looking at him, bewildered, not comprehending what he was talking about and started to protest. But after seeing his raised arm and evil look in his eyes, I thought better of it. I did not want a repeat from the other morning. I turned and ran up the stairs to my room, *sans* dinner, taking two steps at a time, and slammed the door harder than I intended. My windows rattled in their frames, and I was scared that this might bring him flying into my room—but, nothing. I locked my door just in case and flopped on my bed, puzzled by what had just happened. I frantically opened my night side table to make sure the ring and fingernail were still safely tucked in their box and was relieved when I found them just where I had left them. What was I supposed to have done that warranted that kind of punishment, or was it just the alcohol talking? Surprisingly, I noticed I really didn't care. I was becoming calloused to his outbursts. I had more pressing matters at hand to lose any more precious time worrying about it.

CHAPTER 25

JONATHAN

I fell asleep and had the sweetest dream about Chris and Alexa. The dream, for some crazy reason, spanned over time. They were young, in love, straight out of college, and embarking on their dream jobs while planning a family. The best part of all is that they had a dog. He was a Weimaraner named Reggie, with long floppy ears, fur that felt like velvet, with the cutest little white dot right between his eyes that looked like a bindi. I couldn't get enough of him. Chris had become my soccer coach, and they both had taken me under their wing and become my confidants as well as my saviors. We had family dinners where Reggie curled up by my feet, waiting for a handout, and played board games in front of the fire. Trips to the beach and mountains and making each other laugh so hard that we snorted and our drinks came out our noses. It was a big slice of heaven for me and quite a contrast from my present, everyday nightmare of a life. When I woke up, I was smiling and felt all warm inside. I tried my hardest to go back to sleep, because I was so happy and felt so much love, but I couldn't. It made sense that I had dreamt about them, and visualizing them had lit a fire under me more intense than before, if possible. I needed to go exploring to give Chris closure and Alexa redemption. I owed this to "my friends"!

As I peeked through my blinds, I could see that it was still dark and that a light drizzle was coming down. Super Mario told me it was 3:15, which would give me a decent amount of time to do some digging around before school started. That's assuming I was going, which seemed unlikely once again. I still looked like a sight and felt an urgency to unearth more evidence rather than sit in a classroom when my mind was elsewhere. As I crept downstairs, the air seemed heavy, like a dark cloud had descended over the house and was sucking the good air out and replacing it with evil. My tummy growled loud enough to wake the dead, but first things first. I loaded my pockets with an apple, cheese and a peanut butter sandwich. I strapped a camelback over my jacket, put on my gloves and hiking boots, also remembering my beanie and a small shovel my Mom had used to garden with, right as I was sneaking out the back door. I was ready and willing to uncover what deep, dark secrets were lurking in the forest.

The forest seemed ominous tonight. The new information I had acquired, along with my tangible evidence, made the trees seem scary, like they were hiding a gruesome secret. A secret—if I had anything to do with it—was going to be uncovered and justice served. Even though I had been here numerous times, it still scared me. The darkness, the vast number of trees, the silence all added to why it seemed so forbidding to me. The munching on my apple was echoing through the trees, and they seemed to sway with every bite. I couldn't shake the feeling that I was being watched, and this terrified me even further. I was able to find my way to the campfire spot easier this time, following the broken branches and trampled earth as I had before. The metallic smell was stronger the closer I got to the campfire, which concerned me. *Was I closer to death here?* I wondered. I made myself a pallet of pine needles and sat down to finish my meal and formulate a game plan.

My main objective today would be to try to find more evidence of foul play. I was starting to visualize the dreaded night but needed more. Way more. After my countless hours on the internet yesterday, I felt that there was a pattern the psycho killer was following. Young adult women, either out for a jog or nightly walk, during fall or winter months, and alone. The fall and winter months in the Pacific Northwest were generally too cold, rainy and undesirable for a lot of people to be out and about, so the forest would be all but deserted, making it the perfect backdrop for the killer to lie in wait. My imagination was in overdrive now, and I was not only seeing the victims but also the killer, and, to my amazement, he looked nothing like the scary man. He would have to be quick on his feet and nimble. The scary man was neither of these things. Had I been too quick to judge and assume the worst of an innocent man because he was in the wrong place at the wrong time, just like me?

I wasn't going to limit my search to only the campfire spot tonight, because, if my hunch was correct, the killer had been using the whole forest as his playground. This was going to take discipline and precision on my part if I wanted to do the search justice. I knew myself all too well and was positive that, if I found something in one spot, I would get so excited I would not exhaust my search there before running off to explore somewhere else. Fueled and ready to finish my campfire exploration, I noticed the ashes had been shifted around. It was as if someone or something had been rooting in them. I figured a varmint would be attracted to the smell of blood, so this didn't alarm me too much. But what did alarm me was the position of the stones surrounding the ashes. As I got down on my hands and knees, I noticed numerous stones were askew. They were heavy, so this definitely could not have been the work of a forest creature.

Again, I couldn't shake the fact that eyes were watching me. I turned to my left, and, hovering above me was the scary man and Sydney.

CHAPTER 26

JONATHAN

They had the upper hand since I was on my knees and they were standing. I contemplated crawling but decided that was foolish, and I slowly got up with my hands in the air, like a criminal caught in the act. Sydney looked like she wanted to play but sat obediently still at her owner's side. He looked at me and started to chuckle. His chuckle turned into a guffaw that shook his robust belly. I wasn't sure if he was making fun of me or the situation, but listening to him and watching how animated he had become made me smile. Actually it was more of a smirk but kind of an icebreaker all the same. Before I knew it, we were both laughing until tears streamed down our cheeks, as Sydney looked on like we had both lost our minds. In all seriousness, there was nothing about the current situation that was funny, and I felt like I had just disrespected the dead, but there's just something about a laugh that's contagious. After we both had come to our senses, we looked at each other with skepticism. Honestly, I was still a little frightened of him and had many unanswered questions starting with the all-important obvious one: Why was he in the forest in the middle of the night? He towered over me and made me feel smaller than my 5'6" stature. As he extended his callused, gigantic hand to me, I had a split-second decision to make, but, after a second's hesitation, I shook it. It felt warm and welcoming. He spoke first, and when he did, it was soothing and calm. I immediately felt more at ease but was still not willing to let my guard down and become his next victim. I needed answers—and fast—or I would be gone like the wind in two seconds flat. "My name is Luke, and I'm pleased to meet you finally. Why did you run from me yesterday morning, son? I might look scary, but believe me, I'm as gentle as a dove." Why *had* I run, and did I want to tip my hand this early in case his actions were all a façade?

There was something about the gentleness in his voice and the kindness in his eyes, along with my vulnerable state, that made me trust him. I took after my Mom in this department and considered myself a good judge of character, wanting to give him a chance to explain himself. If Sydney liked him, he must not be *that* bad, after all. First I owed him an explanation as to why I had run before I asked him what on Earth he was doing here. I would have to choose my words very carefully, for one, because I didn't want to hurt his feelings, but also because I didn't want to accuse him of something so heinous as chopping someone up when he was possibly innocent.

"Pleased to meet you Luke, I'm Jonathan. Honestly, I'm not entirely positive why I ran," I answered. "The forest scares me, and when I saw you with the severed leg, I assumed the worst." He hung his head, and, when he looked up, anguish washed across his face. He hesitated and answered, "I can explain, and I promise you I was as shocked as you when I saw it. I tried to tell you, but you ran away so fast I couldn't keep up. For years I have been investigating strange happenings in the forest, and that night, I heard the most blood-curdling scream, so I followed it. Imagine my disgust and surprise when I found that leg."

I don't know why, but for some unexplained reason, I believed him. Was it because I was so lonely and needed someone to talk to, or was it his eyes? They were so genuine and trustworthy. As I contemplated my next thought, out of nowhere, the trees began to bend and shake, and a freezing-cold rain fell down in sheets. This conversation would have to continue when we were safe, because it was as if we had accidentally woken the dead, and they were pissed. Now more than ever, I felt a presence of others watching, listening and begging for answers and justice.

This was spooky, to say the least, but also exactly what I needed to once and for all uncover the forbidding secrets lurking within the shadows of the ginormous trees.

I knew as long as the rain was falling as hard as it was, the forest would turn into nothing but a mud bog, making it near impossible to explore. The forest had taken on a ghostly, creepy aura that made me second-guess my sense of adventure. I could tell I wasn't the only one who felt it, because I saw Luke shudder and pull his coat tighter around himself. Sydney was on edge, and her ears were pinned down next to her face with her tail tucked tight under her. She began to bark and turn in circles. That's all we needed to get the hell outta Dodge and head for Luke's cabin.

CHAPTER 27

JONATHAN

As I took off in a full sprint with Sydney by my side, Luke trailed significantly behind, noticeably limping. The sky had really opened up, accompanied by a brisk wind, which made the temperature drop like a stone. By the time we reached the cabin, we were all soaked to the bone and frozen solid. I have never been so happy to feel the warmth of indoors in my life. At first glance, Luke's cabin looked rugged and rustic. An open-beam ceiling and a rock fireplace spanning the length of the wall drew my attention immediately. The place felt homey, with overstuffed maroon chairs and a plaid color-coordinated couch that looked big enough to seat ten. A calico cat stretched lazily in the middle of the couch and welcomed me with a weak *meow* before curling up in a little ball. The walls were semi-sparse, which allowed the wood to show and added to the charm. Directly in front of the fireplace was a big, round, fluffy dog bed with SYDNEY stitched on to its cover. As I looked around, I found one thing that seemed very odd.

There was not a single photograph in a frame anywhere. Either Luke had no family, or he didn't claim the one he had.

I was embarrassed to see that I had created quite a large puddle under me, soaking into the hardwood floor, as I began to thaw out. I was so taken in with my surroundings that I hadn't even noticed Luke standing over me with the biggest, fluffiest towel I had ever seen and a stack of clothes to change into. I was shown into the bathroom, which had a heated toilet seat, a gigantic rainfall shower and an enormous claw-foot tub situated under a paneled window that overlooked the forest to the east and a massive amount of land to the west. I could see some chicken coops set up and a crazy amount of chickens scurrying here and there, trying to get under cover. There was a fenced-in large area that housed a red barn, and I saw horses with multi-colored jackets roaming about. A little further in the distance, there were cows huddled together and what looked like alpacas. A large area had been set aside for two different gardens. One was growing a variety of vegetables and the other a mixture of brightly colored gorgeous flowers. I was really starting to like this place! The clothes I had been given were massive, and to say I was swimming in them wouldn't be an understatement, but they were dry, warm and much appreciated. I rolled them up multiple times and came out looking dry and refreshed. A fire had been started, and on the coffee table sat a mug of steaming hot chocolate and a plate of chocolate-chip cookies. A feeling of contentment I hadn't felt in a long time overpowered me, and it felt good. Really good.

Time stood still as we got to know one another. I quickly became invested in his life's story and hung on every word as he became animated talking about his past. Luke had indeed lived a colorful life, filled with adventure and heartache. I was fascinated as he described his time serving in the military and his deployment to Saudi Arabia during the Gulf War. Sadness washed over his face as he described in great depth the loss of some of his comrades while in battle. He paid a high price himself after returning home, when he became inflicted with Gulf War Syndrome, now suffering from a multitude of debilitating symptoms. His limp was a souvenir from the war, but he wasn't bitter. He'd served his country proudly, and this made me like him more. Unfortunately, because of his dedication to his country, he had severe PTSD, and his beloved Sydney had become his saving grace as his therapy dog. Tears streamed down his cheeks when he told me he was a widower and had no other family, or at least none that claimed him any longer. He had always been a bit of a black sheep of the family, and they had disowned him when he became an alcoholic. He had been down the rabbit hole many times, and it got harder and harder every time to dig his way out. The only way he found to deal with it was by reaching for the bottle to dull his pain both physically and emotionally. His family had given up on him in his deepest, darkest days, and he had become an outcast, forced into solitude.

The parallels between our lives were uncanny. The biggest difference, though, was that Luke realized his downfalls and got help. He struggled daily but was proud that he had been sober for one year now. As I listened intently, my eyes became heavier and heavier until I finally gave in to the sleepiness. I woke up hours later, curled up under a weighted blanket in a very comfy bed in the loft. Between my legs was Sydney on one side and the calico, Buffy, on the other. The feelings of pure contentment enveloped me as I wondered if this is what heaven felt like. As I tried to clear the cobwebs, I couldn't help but savor the moment. For the first time in a long time, I didn't have a nightmare. I was warm and content, but, most importantly, I felt secure.

While I had slept, Luke had been busy making a steaming pot of hearty, homemade beef stew with the little potatoes and chunks of carrots accompanied by a loaf of the best-smelling homemade sourdough bread. His kitchen was a chef's dream with every gadget imaginable.

There were red-and-white-gingham checked curtains hanging around a window that was situated over a farmhouse sink. The window faced to the west as well, and I could see the horses frolicking in the rain. In the middle of the kitchen was a knotty-pine pedestal table with seats for four. The table had been carefully set with red placemats and a bright floral napkin next to the soup bowl, and a vase of freshly picked flowers sat in the middle. I hadn't realized how hungry I was until the steam of the stew wafted through my nose and I began to salivate. I don't know if the meal was the best I've ever tasted because it was just that good or because he had taken the time and effort to make it for me. It had been more than thirteen months since anyone had taken care of me, and it felt incredibly wonderful.

I felt like the whole day so far had been a dream, and I was euphoric, living on cloud nine. "How was your nap?" Luke inquired as I devoured my stew and watched the butter melt on my crusty bread. "I hope you don't mind that I took the liberty of carrying you upstairs so you could be more comfortable. You looked like you needed the rest." Mind, I thought to myself, *You must be kidding me—I loved the attention and thoughtfulness!* But I nonchalantly answered that it was fine and that I appreciated his efforts. For some reason, I couldn't explain, even to myself; I was holding back. Afraid of being hurt perhaps? Or still not letting my guard down completely because I had reservations?

After our tummies were full, we resumed our conversation, sitting in front of a roaring fire, but this time, I was the one doing the talking. Sydney curled up on my feet, keeping them toasty warm while Buffy stretched in Sydney's bed. I started slowly at first, not knowing where to start, but mostly not sure I had the nerve to relive my nightmare. There was so much heartache, and, as I talked about the accident, I was left in a puddle of tears. Luke came and sat next to me, put his arm around my shoulders, and offered me the comfort I had been craving. The comfort my Dad should have given me but refused to. This one small gesture gave me the strength to tell it all—the good, the bad and the ugly. It was therapeutic, and, after I'd let it all out there, I felt exhausted. I shared information about my Dad I hadn't even come to terms with in hopes that some light could be shed on my Dad's erratic behavior—from one alcoholic to another. Luke was a good listener and only interrupted me to offer support or condolences, and I found myself appreciating him, but, more importantly, trusting him.

CHAPTER 28

JONATHAN

I was shocked to see that the sun had set and that it was past ten. I didn't want to go home.

Home just didn't seem like home anymore, and I dreaded what might happen if my Dad found out I had ventured out when I was grounded. I didn't want to tell him about Luke, the cabin or my forest suspicions. Not only would he not believe me, but he wouldn't care. This was something Luke and I could explore together. Two minds were always better than one. Luke and I had decided that we would share our notes on the forest next time we met up. We were both eager to dive right in and get to the bottom of this madness. We both had our suspicions, and I was relieved that I didn't have to face the forest alone ever again.

Saying goodbye proved harder than I thought—a true testament to Luke's character that I already felt comfortable and appreciated here. In such a short period of time, it seemed more like home than my home. I found it so strange to think that, not even a week ago, I had come face to face with Luke and was scared half out of my mind. Now he was my friend, my confidant and my partner in crime—even though we were the two who would be solving the crime, with any luck. Luke insisted I let him drive me home. He said it was too late and not safe to be out alone, on top of the fact there were still threatening clouds just waiting to burst. Of course, he was 100% correct, but it was a foreign feeling to have someone care. But it was amazingly wonderful all the same.

As we turned onto my street, I started to panic. My anxiety had been getting pretty bad lately, and this newest tirade by my Dad had only intensified it. Every time I had started to accept this way as my new normal—becoming callous to his drinking and outrageous behavior—he surprised me and stooped to a new low. Luke must have either heard my heart beating out of my chest or sensed that I was on the verge of losing it because he reached over and put his big, strong, warm hand on my knee. It surprised me that such a small gesture could calm me and mean so much. The house was dark and looked sinister, but I took a deep breath, thanked Luke for his hospitality, and made a date to meet up at his house tomorrow, after school. I figured I'd better make an appearance at school, or they'd come looking for me, and that would open a very unwelcome can of worms. Now that I had a full belly and a weight lifted off my shoulders, having discussed my past thirteen months, I was hopeful I could sleep peacefully in my rainbow room.

As I approached the front door, I had a sense that something was wrong. Everything seemed to be in place. My rocking chair was still on the front porch, moving ever so slightly when the wind hit it just so. I went to sit for a second just to collect my thoughts when I saw it. My new bike was lying in the boxwood hedge that adorned the front of the house. I immediately got up to remove it, and that's when I noticed it had been destroyed. It was missing the handlebars, and both tires had been slashed. I sat on the grass, holding it in my lap, getting soaked, not knowing if it was from my tears or the rainfall. Why would he do such a hurtful thing when he knew how excited I was with it? Or is that why he did it, because he knew this and wanted to hurt me more?

CHAPTER 29

JONATHAN

The house was quiet and musty smelling. The air seemed heavy and difficult to breathe. Was this something new, or had I just accepted it as my new norm and had become accustomed to it? I tiptoed up to my room, stopping at every stair and holding my breath. After seeing my bike in such a sorry state, I was afraid of what might happen to me. As I made it up to my room, I saw that there was note taped to the door. With shaking hands, I read, SORRY THAT IT HAD TO COME TO THIS, BUT DON'T DISRESPECT ME AGAIN. MAYBE YOU'LL LISTEN NEXT TIME!!! It couldn't have been from anyone except my Dad, even though I wished otherwise. I was having a hard time grasping how we had come to this and a harder time seeing how we would find our way out. I started to panic again and immediately ran to my night side table. Everything seemed to be in place, and I let out a huge sigh of relief as I held my box and papers in my hand. I needed to find a better hiding place and decided I would tuck them safely into my backpack and take them to Luke's for safekeeping.

Surprisingly, my night's sleep was uneventful. I had tried my best to put my Dad out of my mind and instead visualized myself running through Luke's pastures, being chased by Sydney, horseback riding, followed by a bubble bath in the enormous tub. I woke up a little nervous about returning to school, but knowing I didn't have a choice gave me the strength I needed to get ready so I wouldn't be late. My eye was still pretty colorful, but the swelling had diminished considerably, so I was pretty sure I wouldn't stand out in a crowd any longer. The house was quiet and cold enough to see my breath when I made my way downstairs at 7 a.m. I was hoping my dad was sleeping off his latest bender and wouldn't show his face, and I got my wish. I managed to make it out the door without a confrontation, and I hoped this was a good omen for the day.

The day was beautiful. The storm of yesterday had given way to sunshine and the cleanest air. No matter which way you looked, you could see for miles and miles. Miles of beautiful, snow-peaked mountains and trees upon trees. My school sat at the top of a hill, surrounded by gigantic redwoods and a creek flowing and winding around, acting as a partial moat. It was reasonably small by comparison to what I had seen on TV and in the movies, but, then again, Mount Sierra was a small town. I went to Mountain View High School, and our mascot was a Rainbow Trout. I had aspirations when I was little that, when I grew up, I would represent the school and wear that goofy costume to all the sporting events. The thirteen-year-old me cringed at the idea and found it embarrassing and just plain silly, even though the meaning behind it made sense. The many streams we had running throughout our little town drew anglers from near and far to compete in numerous fishing competitions The fish, especially rainbow trout, were plentiful, and the scenery was breathtaking.

My school had one main building that served as a lunch-room, auditorium and gymnasium along with a soccer/football/track field that was green and lush, but it was just for practice, as we didn't have any stands for spectators. I would often stare at it and crave the excitement of using my bionic leg and scoring goals as I played soccer, but that was before everything had changed.

Soccer reminded me of my Mom, and the memories were too painful, so I gave it up. My classes were monotonous, and I basically just went through the motions because I had to. I did remember to thank my biology teacher about the lecture on blood, but when he said, "You're welcome," he had a concerned look on his face, so I dropped the subject before I raised suspicions and hurried away. As I went about my day, I realized I was enjoying being out of the house and away from my Dad, but school was boring. I had trouble concentrating and counted down the minutes until I could meet up with Luke and compare notes on the forest and what secrets were buried there. I could feel it in my bones that I was onto something. Something big. Something bigger than big that could rock Mount Sierra to its core once the truth was exposed. Now that I had befriended Luke, I knew we would figure it out once and for all. The day dragged on, but, to my amazement, not one person asked where I had been or commented about my eye. That only reaffirmed what I already knew . . . that nobody gave two hoots about me.

CHAPTER 30

LUKE

My life on the farm was peaceful and lonely at times. The loneliness came mostly at night, when I was alone and left with my memories. Happy memories of a love lost and equally sad memories of a tortured soul. I tried hard to erase the bad times in my life and concentrate on the good, but, somehow, they always resurfaced, tormenting and mocking me. Staying away from the bottle was a constant struggle but one I was determined to conquer. I have been sober for one year now, and I'm proud of the man I have become.

My childhood years were uneventful. I grew up in a small town in Vermont. Open land, clean air and no opportunities. I was never the popular kid in school and was bullied throughout those years, not knowing at the time this would contribute to my alcoholism. I tried to turn the other cheek and pretend that it didn't bother me, but it did. I spent many a night crying myself to sleep, wishing that other kids liked me and wanted to be my friend. My wish never came to fruition, though. So, I struggled through my school years unhappy, alone and the black sheep of my family. I had two brothers who were both star football players and homecoming kings, but, somehow, I was overlooked when good looks and personality were handed out. I was good at feeling sorry for myself, but that's about it. My brothers were best friends and had so much in common, while I, on the other hand, couldn't relate to them in the least. Many a Friday night, while the rest of the family went to the football games, I stayed alone in my room, dreaming about what it would be like to be included.

All of this changed when I met my wife, Claire. We met unexpectedly—at a laundromat, of all places. I rescued her when her long, beautiful auburn hair got caught in the agitator of the washing machine as she was bending down to dislodge some clothes. It was a crazy scenario, and everybody thought we had made it up, but nobody could make that stuff up! I was immediately drawn to her beauty and asked her out on the spot. The rest, as they say, was history. We got married at the local courthouse with only family present. She was an only child, and her parents never thought anyone was good enough for their precious daughter. But I was bound and determined to prove them wrong. Unfortunately, I never got that chance.

Life with Claire was everything I ever wanted and then some. She was the perfect wife in every way, and we spent every second together enjoying each other's company and building memories. Long road trips, where we laughed until we cried, and afternoons spent building sandcastles at the beach. We dreamed about a family to spoil, but we never got the chance before Claire died suddenly of a brain aneurysm. I was distraught beyond words and couldn't believe God could be so cruel to give us only four perfect years together. These were my darkest of days, and I began to drink. A glass of wine here and there, a six-pack of Coronas, and, before I knew it, I was losing control. An intervention was staged by my family, which led me to join the Army. One of the best decisions of my life. I got my life back on track and quickly learned how to toe the line.

For the first time in my life, I felt like I belonged somewhere. I had friends. Real friends who didn't question me but instead accepted me just as I was. The camaraderie and discipline were what I had craved but didn't realize what a difference it would make on the man I would become. I actually enjoyed being told what to do, because, to me, it felt like someone cared. I flourished under their guidance, and for the first time since Claire passed, I was happy and was given a new lease on life. And then the Gulf War happened. Things got crazy, and there was talk of deployments that, truthfully, frightened me a little, but I was all about protecting my country—so, if they needed me, I would be there. I got my orders on November 29, 1990, that I was being deployed to Saudi Arabia in December and to get my finances and will in order. On December 15,1990, I flew into Saudi Arabia with my platoon. The land was vastly different from what I was used to. No matter which way you looked, from east to west or north to south, there was sand. It was a true desert area where we were stationed, with no lakes or rivers to be found. I was hoping for a white Christmas, but that was not in the cards, with temperatures rarely falling below 56 degrees that winter.

Being in the war allowed me to meet various men from other countries that joined us as our allies. Things heated up on January 16, 1991, when the air campaign of Operation Desert Storm started, while back in the States, thousands protested the United States' attack on Iraq. Things got real for me on February 23, when the ground assaults began. I was part of an infantry unit that was sent to the front lines. Those were some of my darkest days as I fought for my country and my life, while I witnessed my friends dying around me. Thank God a ceasefire was called on March 3, before more lives were lost. I learned a lot of valuable lessons while abroad but was never so happy as I was to touch down on American soil on March 8th.

Unfortunately my time served left me with nightmares and Gulf War Syndrome. I struggled with readjusting to life in the States and missed my wife desperately. I was alone once again and began to drink and wallow in self-pity. At first, when I would have memory lapses and fatigue, I was concerned, but as this continued and I also began to experience joint pain, dizziness and respiratory disorders, I dug deeper for answers. This is when I was diagnosed. The next years of my life were pure hell. In and out of veterans hospitals for a variety of ailments. I began drinking more.

Another intervention by my so-called family that wasn't successful. A DUI here and a DUI there, and time behind bars did nothing to change my behavior. I had jobs along the way. I had and still have a green thumb, and I could build anything from the ground up. I loved animals and found them so therapeutic. I got a therapy dog to help me cope with my life. She was a beautiful yellow Labrador Retriever named Cali. She was my best friend and my saving grace. I had glimmers of my old self with her as my constant companion, but I continued to struggle. The last straw with my family was when I was on a bender and crashed my car into a pole, injuring some pedestrians walking nonchalantly down the street. My family turned their backs on me once and for all and said I was a lost cause. Harsh words to hear, even though I had always felt that way about myself. Luckily, nobody was killed that night, and I sobered up while serving more time.

This is a time in my life I don't talk about, not even to Jonathan, my new friend. Once I was released, I decided I would start fresh and move out west to a small quaint town in Oregon named Mount Sierra. I found a huge piece of land with 10 acres and the perfect cabin to call home. The year was now 2010, and Cali had long since passed, so I once again found myself in need to surround myself with animals. I built a chicken coop and a big red barn on my property and filled it with chickens, horses, cows and alpacas. I was happy for the first time in a long time. I picked up odd jobs here and there as a handyman, but the bulk of my money had come from an inheritance from my grandparents that I got once I had turned 25. Life continued at a slow pace, and I still struggled with my pains and nightmares, but I busied myself with life on the farm. I was finally content and had found my little slice of heaven.

It was about 2014 when I started hearing screams and cries for help that sounded desperate coming from the east side of my property, where the forest started. It had me so concerned that I would investigate on my own late at night. The forest was always dark, damp and downright creepy, but I didn't let that deter me. I had my suspicions that some very horrendous, unthinkable things were going on. A couple of times, I had seen where the ground had been moved around like there had been a struggle, and dirt that had been made into mounds. There was always the oddest smell that I couldn't put my finger on, and I attributed it to the dampness. Through the years, I had accumulated a little collection of odds and ends I'd found during my investigative trips. A blue baseball cap with the Nike swoosh embroidered on the front, a pink ribbon, a pair of glasses, a multicolored beaded bracelet, a gold hoop earring and an AirPod—until the other night when

I found the severed leg. In my heart, I knew I should turn these belongings and my suspicions over to the police, but, in all honesty, I was scared that this would bring unwanted attention to me and dig up the past I had left behind.

Fast forward to 2018. I got a new therapy dog. This time it was a golden retriever, and I named her Sydney. I felt myself starting to slip a little, and I needed a companion once again. My pain was coming more frequently and more intensely, and the demons started to rear their ugly heads. I wasn't one to take medications, so, instead, I drank to ease the pain. My worst nightmare came true in the fall of 2018. I had gone to a bar out of town for a change of scenery and was too drunk to drive home. My judgment was impaired, and I jumped into a car with a guy I had been talking sports with, thinking he was fine to drive. Turns out he wasn't, and we got into a fatal car accident that night. I wasn't hurt, and the other guy, whose name I didn't even bother to ask, had scrapes and bumps but was well enough to walk away. But, to my horror, he killed a young mother, and her son witnessed the whole thing. He was dressed in soccer cleats and shin guards, so I assumed he was going home from soccer practice. I can still hear his screams as he hovered over his mother, begging her to wake up. The rest of the night was a blur. After that night and the scare of my life, I joined AA and have been sober ever since.

I was terrified after hearing Jonathan's story yesterday and thinking that I might have contributed to his mother's death. Could it have inadvertently been my fault? Am I partially responsible for ripping this young boy's life apart? It just seems too coincidental, but I couldn't bear to bring it up. I am in such a solid spot in my life and feel a kinship with Jonathan, so I'm hoping and praying that it isn't so. I put it out of my thoughts for the time being and instead busied myself for my meeting with Jonathan.

CHAPTER 31

JONATHAN

I made it through the day, and, as soon as the final bell rang, I was out in a flash. Luke would be waiting, and time was wasting. Making sure my backpack with my hidden treasures was firmly in place, I took off in a full sprint and didn't stop until I reached the outskirts of Luke's property. I purposely avoided the forest and went the long way, because my spidey senses were once again telling me danger was lurking in there. Now that Luke and I were a team, we would tackle it together, with the help of Sydney to thwart off any bad people we might encounter. God willing, we wouldn't come face to face with anyone, but we needed a plan in place just in case luck wasn't on our side. Standing there, looking toward the cabin, I tried to catch my breath. A peaceful calm washed over me that I hadn't felt at home in a while. There was something about the property that enveloped me in warmth and contentment. It seemed odd to me that I would feel this way so quickly, but I welcomed it all the same. Luke had a way about him that made me feel comfortable and cared for. After hearing his life's achievements and failures—and he mine—it felt like we had always known each other and were kindred spirits.

I was startled out of my thoughts when Sydney jumped up and planted a big juicy kiss right across my face. I was just as happy to see her as she obviously was to see me! I looked up and saw Luke standing on his front porch, waving, with a big goofy smile on his face. As I got closer, a familiar smell permeated the air and made me ravenous. I was transported back to the kitchen at home, eating one of my Mom's sugar cookies warm and straight out of the oven. The smell of vanilla and cinnamon always got me and flooded me with memories. A lone tear ran down my cheek before I could wipe it away or turn away from Luke. I was embarrassed and vulnerable but relieved when Luke offered me his handkerchief. He folded me into his arms, and I experienced the biggest bear hug that left me weak in the knees and thankful. After I collected myself, we sat in front of the fire, eating his fresh homemade snickerdoodles and making small talk. Small talk kept us from addressing the elephant in the room, because we both knew that once we opened that door, it would be all consuming, and we would not close it until justice was served.

When I returned from washing up and making a small pit stop to pet Buffy as she sprawled in a sunbeam coming through the window, I was excited to see that Luke had prepped a spot at the kitchen table for us to dig in. Off to the left side sat a box with what looked like a pink ribbon peeking out of the top. There were hand-drawn renderings of the forest scattered about, and a neatly piled stack of maps was sitting next to the box. Rounding out the table to the right side sat a massive plate of apple nachos. How he knew they were one of my favorite snacks was beyond me, but I could hardly wait to dig into the slices of apples covered in caramel and sprinkled with finely chopped peanuts and shredded coconut. To say I was ecstatic wouldn't begin to describe how I was feeling. Great company, yummy snacks and digging into our "souvenirs" was the highlight of my day. I couldn't contain myself—I let out a gleeful shriek as I ran to grab my backpack. As I unloaded my box and research, my excitement grew.

I let Luke talk first, partially because I was interested in what he had acquired through the years as well as his suspicions, but mostly because I was too excited to talk. I was mesmerized as he laid out all the belongings he had found in the forest. Each one had been found after a night of screams he had heard ranging back to 2014. As I dug through my research, I discovered that I was correct—the women had started going missing in 2014. This was not a coincidence; of that, I was 100% sure. There was a deranged lunatic running amok in Mount Sierra, and we needed to take him/her down.

I noticed when Luke felt passionate about something, he became quite animated. He was definitely passionate about this because his arms were moving up and down and to and fro. He was talking a mile a minute and stopped only to take a quick breath or munch on an apple slice. I had become fixated on his every word and could have listened for hours or quite possibly days.

He described in detail the blood-curdling screams that had led to his investigation. He also noticed the metallic smell in the forest but hadn't put two and two together until I told him what I had researched about blood. We complemented each other well; with his exploration and my research about the last five years, we were able to match the missing women to the items recovered from the forest. The day I had spent holed up in my room doing research came in handy today. After I had read the article in the *Pacific Sun Times* from September 28th regarding Alexa Hopkins, I Googled "missing women in Mount Sierra and adjoining areas from 2014 to present day." At that time, I learned about the other eleven women. Each article described in detail when the women had gone missing and what they had been wearing and doing the last time they had been seen. This gave us the opportunity to assign the objects found in the forest to an actual person. Somehow, in a weird way, it humanized them and made me feel even closer to them. This made me more motivated than ever to want to be part of putting an end to this madness that had been happening far too long.

In my opinion, these women had suffered a gross injustice because the Mount Sierra Sheriff's Department had dropped the ball not once or even twice, but multiple times. Twelve to be exact. Not one of these crimes had been solved, and they had been sitting in the sheriff's office as cold cases, with the exception of Alexa's case, which I hoped was still actively being investigated. Not only was this an injustice for the women but a complete and utter travesty. Understandably, the department was small and lacked expertise and manpower, but if Luke and I had been able to find evidence with our limited resources, it should have been a cakewalk for them. Their families needed closure, and the poor women needed to rest in peace. I wasn't looking for notoriety, but the sound of the headline in the *Pacific Sun Times*—"Local High School Freshman and Gulf War Veteran Single-handedly Thwart Mass Murderer!" had a special ring to it and made me proud. But, most importantly, I knew my Mom would be proud. The lack of investigating was both inexcusable and appalling, and only reaffirmed what we both thought. We would do this together, keep our mouths shut until we had undeniable proof, and only then would we come forward.

CHAPTER 32

JONATHAN

As we studied the maps and compared them to the drawings Luke had made, we were able to pinpoint where we thought the murders had taken place. We both had a very strong feeling that these women had perished at the hands of this lunatic and not been taken captive. We actually had nothing to go on that could confirm this except our gut instincts. So far, our gut hadn't let us down, so we were all about putting our faith where it belonged. All in all, between the two of us, we had found seven pieces of evidence, excluding the leg. With 100% certainty, we were convinced that the leg and the gold band I had found belonged to Alexa, the latest victim. With the inscription in the ring and the ASICS running shoe attached to the leg, they were a definite match to what her husband Chris said she was wearing. So that meant we had either missed some evidence of the remaining six women or that there just hadn't been any left behind. We once again weighed the possibility that they had been abducted and were being held against their will somewhere, but we excused that idea because it just didn't fit the lunatic's modus operandi.

All the articles I had printed out about the missing women had pictures attached, and we couldn't help but notice the similarities. This lunatic definitely had a type. They were all women between the ages of 25 and 40, with long blonde hair and apparently easy targets out for either a jog or walk on the trail adjacent to the forest. Luke got up from the table, went into the other room and brought back a couple of candles. As we looked at these young women, all smiling and full of life in their prime, we held hands, and Luke led me in a prayer. A prayer that hopefully found them at peace and devoid of any suffering. We made a promise to all of them that their killer would get his comeuppance once and for all if we had to die trying. I was touched that Luke thought to do this and once again reaffirmed my feelings that his heart was made of pure gold.

The sun had set, and, by the time we took a breather, it was 9 p.m. We were so invested in our mission that neither one of us had even noticed our tummies growling and Sydney staring nonstop at us, pleading for her dinner. While I was in school, Luke had prepared a lasagna that he'd popped into the oven; he pulled out a loaf of that crusty, delicious sourdough bread and made a salad with the bounty from his garden. It tasted divine and hit the spot. I was once again surprised and amazed at Luke's hidden talents. We had devised a plan that consisted of starting by the campfire spot first, since it was the most recent crime and our chances of finding evidence were better. After comparing notes, we both came to terms with the danger we were in and decided to stay together with Sydney's help. Even though it was getting late and I should be making an appearance at home, I decided against it. My Dad would just have to get mad at me, assuming he noticed, because getting to the bottom of the forest crisis took precedence. I was positive that there would be another tragedy if we didn't get to the bottom of this whole fiasco, so the sooner the better. Luke had gone on a shopping spree to the local hardware store earlier in the day and stocked up on all kinds of supplies. We had miners' hats, lanterns, shovels and some work gloves for good measure. Also, in pure Luke fashion, he had the foresight to buy a polaroid camera to document anything we might find. He assured me that, if trouble were to present itself, he would not, under any circumstances, allow anything to happen to me. I wasn't sure how he was going to carry this off, but I had a sneaking suspicion that he was packing a gun.

After filling thermoses with hot chocolate and with cookies in my pocket, we locked up the cabin and headed out. It was clear and cold, with a whole sky full of the brightest stars. Just as I looked up to make a wish for luck, I saw one fall from the sky. Legend has it that a shooting star is said to possess a bit of magic, which means positive vibes and good luck to anyone who happens to gaze upon one. Whatever it was, I took it as a good omen. The moon was full and bright, which usually meant the crazies would be out in full force. I hoped this wasn't a precursor to what we might find skulking around. Even though I wasn't superstitious, I was putting a lot of faith in that shooting star, or else I would have called the whole thing off, but, instead, I forged full steam ahead.

CHAPTER 33

JONATHAN

As we approached the forest, the hair on my arms stood up, and I could have sworn I heard voices. I stopped dead in my tracks and tried to focus on the sounds of the night. The night was still and quiet, except for an occasional cricket. The full moon partially illuminated the ground, which created eerie shadows that made me jump and gasp. My sense of adventure had packed up its bags and left for the night, because I was horrified by what I might find. I was not easily intimidated by the forest, but all this talk with Luke had me on edge. Luke sensed my hesitation and gave me a quick thumbs-up as we made our way in.

It made absolutely no difference whatsoever that the moon was full, because, as usual, it was pitch-black. The trees were thick and full at this point, and we had to maneuver our way around to the clearing that had the campfire. I let Luke lead the way, with Sydney trailing close behind me. I could hear her panting as we ventured closer. Oddly, it calmed me down. In case either one of us sensed danger, we had devised a plan to flash our lanterns twice. Other than that, we had decided not to use them until we reached the campfire, just in case we had unwanted company. I second-guessed this decision immediately. I couldn't explain what had me so on edge tonight, but I was more panicked than ever. So panicked in fact that, I didn't even notice that Luke had stopped in front of me until I ran right into him. I couldn't help myself, and I screamed like a little girl. It echoed through the trees and made Sydney bark. So much for us sneaking around unnoticed.

"Luke, what happened? Why did you stop?" I asked.

"I thought I heard a branch snap, so I stopped to listen closer and pinpoint where it had come from" he whispered. We both held our breath, and, sure enough, we were not alone.

The same time we realized we were not alone was the instant I smelled something different than pine needles and damp earth mixed with blood. It was a sweet aroma that smelled like a mixture of french toast and cedar. I recognized it immediately as a high-quality cigar. Not any of those cheap ones you buy at the grocery store but the kind that you buy from Cuba and keep in a humidor. My grandpa used to smoke them a lot, and that's one smell I'll never forget. It was faint but noticeable. Cigars were like that, though: Powerful when being smoked but lingering hours after. Luke and I shared a glance. With all our planning, we had neglected to figure out what we would do if we actually encountered someone. As we stood there still and quiet, my mind raced, and I broke out in a sweat. Sydney stood obediently by Luke's side, waiting for her next command. "Let's wait right here for a spell until we are positive we are in the clear," Luke mumbled, barely audible.

Standing still and quiet proved to be harder than it sounds. I became fidgety, and my throat felt like it constantly needed to be cleared. I couldn't catch my breath, and my breathing was labored and very shallow as I strained to take a deep breath. I knew this feeling all too well. It started the night I watched my Mom pass in front of me. I was starting to have a panic attack, so I needed to get a grip and focus on deep breaths and going to a happy place in my mind. I struggled at first but found my zone after bending down and petting Sydney. I wasn't even sure how much time had passed when Luke tapped me on the shoulder and told me it was time to move. The danger had passed, and he felt confident we were alone and in the clear. I didn't share his optimism but trusted his instincts and went along with him all the same.

As we approached the clearing, the cigar smell grew stronger. The mixture of smells in the air was calming, frightening and nauseating all at the same time. I stayed in my happy place until I had my bearings and felt more secure. The campfire was warm. I found a long stick and poked in the pit. The fire had sufficiently been extinguished, but there were still some burning embers that had survived being snuffed out. It offered a small amount of warmth, and I stood over it, removing my gloves and letting it flood me with memories of the past and camping with my family. Next thing I knew, Sydney was pawing at me, and Luke had his miner's hat on and lantern in hand. No matter how therapeutic my talk with Luke had been the other day, it clearly had opened up a great many emotions I had buried long ago. I just needed a little alone time to sort them out and compartmentalize them so I could focus, and I would be good as new.

Unfortunately things had been moving quickly, and I had not been able to do that yet, so I was in a bit of a fragile state. Therapy dogs were extremely intuitive to this, and Sydney stood glued to my side. I sat down for a minute and buried myself in her fur, allowing myself a tear or two while I hugged and petted her. She gently licked my tears and offered me her paw as she wagged her tail. Sensing my mood, Luke gave me all the time I needed while he dug around and overturned rocks. To say I was grateful for Luke would be an understatement. He knew when to back off and give me space as well when to be there with a big bear hug or consoling words. I needed this in my life more than I realized or wanted to admit. The loss of my Mom and abandonment by my Dad had taken their toll. I finally realized I needed to seek the help that had been offered a while ago but which I had shunned. When I came to the realization that I needed help, it felt like a weight had been lifted from my shoulders. It was time to dive in and help Luke so we could get these poor, unfortunate women the justice they deserved.

CHAPTER 34

JONATHAN

I tiptoed quietly to where Luke was bent over, digging in the dirt, and scared the crap out of him. He jumped, and dirt flew in the air, which lightened the mood considerably, and I couldn't help but crack up. Poor guy. He gave me a big smile and inquired about my mental state. I assured him that I was ready and willing to join him and not to worry. I could tell by his expression that he didn't 100% believe me but decided to let it go for now. "Have you found anything of importance?" I asked. He shook his head "No" and offered me a lantern and a miner's hat. It was time to get busy.

It's easy to lose track of time in the forest because of the darkness and cold temperatures, but I figured about three hours had passed since we'd first heard the branch snap. Time enough for the cigar-smoking stranger to have left but not enough time to make a lot of progress. I wanted more than anything to dive right in, but I was emotionally and physically exhausted, which was making it hard for me to concentrate. The last thing I wanted to do was disappoint Luke—or the women, for that matter—so I took a deep breath and put my big-boy pants on. We had both discussed earlier that we would work together but separate, if that makes sense. We had a lot of ground to cover, so he chose one spot by the campfire, and I chose another, but we made sure never to lose sight of one another. Sydney still sensed my mood and became my constant companion, which I loved.

I chose a spot about twenty-five feet away from Luke under a huge pine tree. I had noticed the ground was uneven and there was a small mound of dirt that looked out of place. I'm not entirely sure what I was looking for, but I knew I'd know it when I saw it. As I was feverishly digging, my shovel hit something hard that made a loud, clanging sound and vibrated the shovel. At first, I thought it was a tree root, but, when I got on my hands and knees and started digging with my hands, I instantly knew I had stumbled onto something. It was hard, like metal, and rectangular-shaped, like a box. I shone my light in the hole I had dug and could see shades of red bouncing back at me, like it was shiny. I frantically started clawing at the dirt surrounding it, so that I could free it from the hole, all the while not quite positive if I was ready for the contents it held. As I freed it from the dirt, I tried with all my might to lift it up, but it was either incredibly heavy or stuck on something. I urgently called out to Luke to come quickly. He ran over with a concerned look on his face, thinking I had hurt myself. Letting him know I was fine and just needed some extra muscle power, he was able to breathe a sigh of relief. We set our lanterns on either side of the hole, and I positioned the flashlight just so, trying to make it easier for Luke to get a good, solid grip—but to no avail. He couldn't lift it, either. Our next step was to try to find out what was causing it to feel like dead weight. We both used our shovels and dug a huge hole surrounding the box, so that we could get entirely underneath it.

That's when we realized that the problem was not that we were weaklings. On the bottom of the box, a chain had been attached, leading to what, we weren't sure yet. It became abundantly clear that someone had gone to great lengths to keep this securely underground, which only added to the intrigue and made us more determined than ever to remove it. After a great deal of grunting and sweating, we uncovered a 100-pound weight attached to a chain that was every bit of ten feet long. Unearthing this was no easy feat, and we both gave each other a pat on the back, while Sydney jumped in the hole, digging to her heart's content.

We were now faced with the dilemma of what to do with this mystery box. There were so many factors, and we were determined not to tip our hand. After a short discussion, we came to the conclusion that whoever had gone to all the trouble of burying the box would most certainly be back to check on it—and, quite possibly, add something else to it. There was a giant padlock that kept us from peeking inside, but that would be an easy fix as soon as we had the proper tools. We decided to mark the spot and cover it up so that the owner would be none the wiser. Covering it up wasn't quite as laborious as digging it out, but we were still exhausted and out of breath. We decided to call it a night and return tomorrow with the proper excavating equipment, along with some bolt cutters. It was going to be a long day, and, hopefully, the anticipation wouldn't get the best of me.

As we were packing up our supplies, Sydney came galloping over with something in her mouth. "What do you have there, girl?" Luke inquired while scratching her head and prying it from her mouth. To our surprise it was a half-smoked cigar. We almost peed ourselves with excitement. This had to be one and the same cigar the stranger had been smoking just hours earlier. The DNA off this was an incredible coup for us, which warranted another pat on the back, followed by a high-five.

The excitement of discovering the box and now the cigar gave us both a charge of adrenaline we hadn't anticipated. After starting to wrap it up for the night, we decided we were on a roll, so what harm would a little more digging do? On my previous excursions into the forest before meeting Luke, I had noticed a variety of areas that all had a random mound of dirt. I was mystified by these, because, for one, they were randomly placed, and, two, they looked man-made. I had been wanting to investigate them, but my Mom's gardening trowel wasn't going to make a dent. So, with Luke and Sydney in tow, we tackled the first one we found. If my memory was serving me correctly, the mounds were all positioned under big Ponderosa Pines like they were being marked with a makeshift headstone of sorts.

The trees in the northwestern terrain of Oregon housed a variety of trees—from Douglas Firs, Big Leaf Maples, Oregon White Oaks, just to name a few, to the massive Ponderosa Pine.

Ponderosa Pines grew to be up to 130' tall and let off a faint smell of butterscotch and vanilla if you cut into their bark; they were beautiful. I couldn't help but think the mounds positioned under these trees was anything other than a coincidence. It didn't take too long, with Luke and me using the shovels and Sydney digging like she was looking for buried treasure, to make headway. We were about to give up, thinking we were on a wild goose chase, when my shovel hit something other than dirt.

I shone my light in there and saw a brown box. It looked to be about a twelve-inch-by-twelve-inch typical cardboard packing box. We reluctantly lifted it out, not wanting to think about what it could contain. It was not heavy and came out easily. As Luke opened the flap, I turned my head, afraid to look. I heard him breathe a sigh of relief, which eased my mind somewhat. Inside was a stack of women's clothes, very neatly folded. I immediately recognized the ones belonging to Alexa Hopkins. Something about seeing her clothes made it real to me. In the back of my mind, I knew she had suffered a tragic death, but my heart still hoped I was wrong. Now I had to accept the fact that this was worse than we ever could have imagined. We took pictures and folded the clothes neatly before replacing them into the box where they now lived. What had the killer been thinking when he disrobed his victims and folded their clothes so neatly? Had he known his victims, or was he just some kind of neat freak with a weird fetish? My mind was filled with unanswered questions that left me feeling unhinged and repulsed. We both agreed this was as much heartache as we could absorb in one night and packed up for the night.

Clearly, time had gotten away from us while digging around, because, when we emerged, the roosters were squawking up a storm, and the sun was starting to peek over the mountaintops. The mountaintops were sprinkled with termination dust, leading me to believe that winter would be arriving sooner than expected. Although fall was my favorite month, I usually looked forward to winter as well. I used to love Christmas when my Mom was still alive. Every year on the first of December, she would drive me to school and immediately came home and transposed our home into a winter wonderland. Lights twinkled from every imaginable space, and mistletoe hung jauntily over the threshold. It was family tradition for us to cut down our own tree from the local Christmas tree farm the day after Thanksgiving. I looked forward to it every single year as we walked up down the rows, singing "Oh Christmas Tree," while looking for the perfect tree. Amazingly, we always found one even better than the perfect tree from the year before. The rest of the evening was spent drinking hot chocolate and listening to Christmas carols as we decorated the tree with colorful bright lights, handmade clay snowmen, candy canes and Santas, along with various bulbs that sparkled when the lights hit them. We popped our own popcorn over the fire and strung it carefully to make garlands. It was a magical time that always made me feel warm and fuzzy. My Mom had passed about three months prior to Christmas last year, so, needless to say, it was disastrous, and the way my Dad was acting lately, I didn't hold high hopes for this Christmas, either. But I could hope. I always had hope in my back pocket.

To Luke's dismay, I called dibs for the shower as soon as we walked through the door. We were both covered from head to toe in dirt, and pine needles had somehow found their way into his beard and my hair. We were a sight and couldn't stop laughing at how funny we both looked. It felt so good to laugh. It had been so long since I'd had something to laugh about that I was afraid I had forgotten how.

CHAPTER 35

MICHAEL

I'm not sure it was possible for me to hate myself any more than I did. My erratic behavior was mimicking Dr. Jekyll and Mr. Hyde, and I wasn't sure which personality would rear its ugly head next. Quite frankly, it frightened me. My drinking needed to stop immediately, but, as soon as I became sober, the hurt of losing Emma crushed my soul. I found my thoughts wandering to the start of our love story and how it developed through the years into something novel-worthy. It was the happiest I had ever been, and feeling her reciprocate my feelings made it all that much better. Life was perfect in every way, and then she was killed. The life I knew and loved was gone in the blink of an eye.

I'm scared to do this life without her. She was the life of the party, while, I, on the other hand, am shy and pretty much socially inept. Not to sound cheesy, but she was the glue that kept our family together and running like a well-oiled machine. Now all I had were the broken parts that were falling apart. And I was the main contributor to its demise. Jonathan tried, but I was making it almost impossible for him to love me anymore. How could I expect anyone to love me when I didn't even love myself?

I knew what I had to do to save my relationship with Jonathan and resurrect life back into our family, but I didn't know how to do it. I had lost all my friends and business acquaintances in the last six months. To their credit, they tried to help, but I constantly pushed them away and made a fool of myself one too many times. There comes a time when everyone has had enough, and they reach their breaking point. I can't say that I blame them. I was despicable and not worthy of love. Truthfully, I would miss the camaraderie, but I didn't crave it like I craved my time with Jonathan. Why had I been so mean lately?

I was scared that he had been through enough and, like my friends, would, once and for all, get tired of trying, leave, and never look back. I couldn't bear it. I know he needs me and misses his Mom as much as I miss her. We need to talk. I want to lay it all out on the table and start to rebuild our relationship. I'm not naive, and I know this will take time and perseverance, but I need to try. The only problem with that is I don't know where he is. I haven't seen him in two days, and I'm worried that my latest tirade was too much. I had been drinking—what else is new?—and my temper got the best of me. The craziest thing about that is I don't have a temper when I'm sober. I actually was quite successful, with a sharp wit, before I found myself wallowing in self-pity and drowning my sorrows in gin.

I walked into Jonathan's room, and it was obvious he hadn't been here. His blinds were drawn, and only a sliver of light shone through, casting shadows in his rainbow room. I remember when he painted this. Emma had told him that, since it was his room, he could do whatever he wanted because it should be an expression of himself. He had done just that and was so proud of it. His backpack, jacket and shoes were gone, but it looked like the majority of his clothes were still hanging neatly in his closet. I noticed his computer lying on the night side table, so I fired it up in hopes it would shed some light on his whereabouts. I opened up Google and brought up his recent searches. My heart stopped when I read that he had been reading about alcoholism. Question after heart-wrenching question . . . What defines an alcoholic? Does alcohol make you mean?

Why do you isolate yourself when you're drunk? Can you still love when you're an alcoholic? How can you help someone who's drinking too much? The list went on and on. As hard as this was to see, it gave me hope and the push I needed. I started doing research of my own and had to ask myself why I hadn't done this before.

I spent the afternoon researching and reading. I felt optimistic that, if I put in the effort, I could come out on the other side and be the man Emma fell in love with and the Dad I used to be.

Jonathan used to look up to me and respect me, but it would be a long haul to get his trust back. I felt accomplished already because I had taken the first step—admitting I had a problem.

Admitting was only the beginning, though. I needed to act on this, or it was all for naught. I wasn't sure that I could conquer this on my own, but I was going to give it the old college try with the help of AA. I knew in my mind that my body had become physically dependent on alcohol, but reading about the withdrawals I could experience, from headaches, shaking, sweating, nausea or vomiting, to trouble sleeping and concentrating—just to name a few—sent fear and doubt through me. I was not going to let this fear cloud my judgment, though. I had to concentrate on the positive, and knowing that the symptoms should start to improve within five days was entirely doable. It would be a small price to pay for a lifetime with Jonathan.

I read that support was essential, hence AA. Having the support from others who understood exactly what I was going through would be crucial in my recovery. Who knows? I might be able to pick up pointers from shared experiences of members and gain a friend along the way. I wrote down goals, short- and long-term, and mapped out how my life would have to change to live a sober lifestyle. From taking better care of myself by eating better, exercising, and getting plenty of sleep. I needed new hobbies that I found fulfilling. Also doing things that gave me a sense of meaning and purpose. It sounded daunting, but there was no better time than the present, and if I took one step at a time, I knew I could accomplish it.

I flew through the house and gathered up every bottle of alcohol that was in plain sight or hidden away. It was almost like a party of sorts, as I poured bottle after bottle down the sink. I felt empowered, and this was something I hadn't felt in a long time. I got the address of the local AA meetings and added the meetings to my calendar; then I sat down to write a heartfelt letter to my son. Today was the first day of my rebirth, and I felt on top of the world.

CHAPTER 36

JONATHAN

The shower was totally euphoric. Who knew warm water could have that effect on you? As rejuvenating as it felt at the time, exhaustion took over immediately. I knew that I was going to have to go back to my house at some point today to pick up more clothes and make sure my Dad hadn't drunk himself into oblivion. I wasn't planning on staying there, though. There was nothing left there for me except heartache and possibly more abuse. Neither of which I was a fan of. Luke had started a roaring fire that warmed the whole place. A plate of French toast with melting butter and a light sprinkling of powdered sugar was sitting next to a plate of crispy bacon and a glass of freshly squeezed orange juice. I could get used to this real quick. As I dug in—hardly chewing but savoring every bite—I started nodding off while sitting up. I finally gave in, laid my head down on my arms, and fell into a deep sleep. Next thing I knew, I woke up 10 hours later in the same bed in the loft where I had taken a nap the other day. And just like the other day, I had my sleeping companions on either side of me, sprawled out and snoring lightly. As I wiped the sleep from my eyes, I tried to remember Luke carrying me up to the loft to sleep the day away, but all I could remember was my dream.

It was about my Dad. I was standing on the porch, looking through a window at him. He was sitting in my favorite brown chair at our house, wrapped in a blanket, shivering and looking like he had been through a war and come out on the losing end. There was a fire in the fireplace and what looked like a cup of coffee was sitting by his side, but he was alone. And sad and possibly sick. I stood contemplating my next move. I wanted to help him but was scared of what might happen. Did he want my help, or would he be mad that I had interfered? Time stood still as I flashed back to all the wonderful camping trips we'd taken as a family, past holidays, and my Saturdays spent with him. Thirteen years of memories condensed into fifteen minutes of time. When I came out of my trance, my Dad was looking right at me. His stare was blank and vacant, and his coloring was awful. His skin looked like wax, with a deathlike pallor. He opened his mouth to speak, but no words came out—just a hollow stare. It was haunting, to say the least, and it left me feeling shaken and uneasy.

The smells of something wonderful awoke my senses, and I padded downstairs with Sydney and Buffy at my heel. "Well, look who the cat dragged in," Luke joked and laughed at his own joke. "I decided to let you sleep today and went out to run a couple of errands." Just then I noticed a note on the table explaining just this and that he would return shortly and to make myself at home if I were to wake in the meantime. Thoughtful as usual, and I was pleased that he had taken the time to jot it down. I had slept through lunch, so the grilled filet mignon with au gratin potatoes and a side of fresh roasted veggies hit the spot. I savored every bite as Luke told me about his day.

While I had been sleeping peacefully—crazy dream and all—he had been busy buying the tools we needed for the mystery box as well as attending an AA meeting and therapy session. I tried to explain my dream, and, when I did, it made me more eager to return home to check on my Dad. For some strange unexplained reason, I couldn't shake the feeling that something was wrong. Luke agreed to drive me home after dinner but only after I caved in and said I would meet with his therapist. It was long overdue and drastically needed. I had to admit to myself that I was looking forward to talking to someone besides Luke about the tragedy that haunts me every day.

CHAPTER 37

JONATHAN

As we drove to my house, we decided to take the night off from the forest, out of caution as well as needing to devise a more in-depth plan. We would resume tomorrow night, after I went to school during the day. I had mixed emotions about this. I was eager to break into the mystery box and uncover what I hoped would be oodles of evidence, but I also needed to regroup in my mind. Even after my marathon sleep, I was bone-tired. As we pulled up in front of my house, it looked lonely. A lone light shone in the family room behind closed shutters, and I hesitated one second too long before opening the car door. Luke reached over and squeezed my knee. "Would you like me to come with you?" he volunteered. As much as I wanted him to, I needed to do this alone whatever the consequences might be. Knowing he would be waiting for me gave me the strength to do what had to be done.

The door was locked, but I removed the spare key we kept safely tucked under the asparagus fern next to the door. The door creaked as I opened it and walked into a different smell. It didn't smell musty and stale, like it had before. I could tell a fire had been burning earlier, but it was more than that. It smelled fresh, like it had been cleaned. As I looked around, taking in my surroundings, I was both shocked and pleased to see everything was in its place. The kitchen was tidy, and a fresh bouquet of the remaining flowers from my Mom's garden were sitting in a vase I had made for Mother's Day when I was in sixth grade. Tucked underneath the vase was a letter addressed to me. I froze, not knowing what to expect. Obviously, it was from my Dad, but its contents were anyone's guess. As my legs grew weak, I sat down at the kitchen table and opened it with trembling hands.

Dear Jonathan,

I'm not sure where to begin because there's so much that needs to be said. So many broken promises on my end, not to mention my behavior. I am appalled and sickened at the man I have become, but I want you to know that I have taken steps to rectify this and become the Dad you once admired and respected. I want you to know that, throughout it all, I never stopped loving you. You and your Mom are the best things that ever happened to me, and losing her put me over the edge. I haven't dealt with it the right way and multiple times taken it out on you. I'm sorry from the bottom of my heart. I know you must hate me, and I don't blame you; I hate myself. I understand if you don't want to have anything to do with me, but I promise you I am changing. I have thrown away all the alcohol so as not to have temptation while I am detoxing. Please try to find it in your heart to give me another chance. I swear—this time, I won't let you down. All I ask is that you give me the time to detox alone because I don't want you to see me like this. I'm worried about you and don't know where you have gone, so please leave me a note if you read this and let me know you're okay.

I love you to Pluto and back,

Dad

I must have sat there deep in thought for at least fifteen minutes. So many emotions were running wild in my head, crashing in to each other. I couldn't make heads or tails of what I was feeling. I desperately wanted to believe him, but I wasn't sure I did. I knew I still loved him—that was for certain—but I had been hurt emotionally, physically and mentally. I didn't want to drop my guard now and end up being let down again. Detoxing wasn't a walk in the park. I had done my research, and, knowing my Dad, I'm sure he had as well. I needed to digest this, but not here. I quietly walked upstairs and listened at his closed door. I heard him talking to himself. "Dad, it's just Jonathan. I got your note and will honor your wishes by letting you be. I'm fine and am staying with a friend. I will come check on you later." His only response was a raspy croak that sounded like "Be safe," but I couldn't be entirely sure. I grabbed clothes, jammed as much as I could into my backpack and locked the door behind me.

Luke was sitting, patiently waiting, in the car, with the heater still running so that I didn't freeze when I got in. Always the thoughtful guy. "Are you okay?" he asked. Surprisingly, I wasn't ready to share the letter. I needed the time to myself to try to decipher its meaning before I talked openly about it. "I'm fine. I would prefer to not talk right now, if that's okay," I answered, on the verge of tears. He nodded his consent and told me when I was ready, he would be more than willing to listen. We rode back to his house in uncomfortable silence. I could feel that he knew something was up but was nice enough not to pry.

The rest of the night was a wash. We made small talk, but I wasn't in the mood and asked if it was okay if I retired early, after eating the hot-fudge sundae he had made with whipped cream and a cherry on top. He offered me the loft, but I declined and said I would rather sleep by the fire. I knew I probably wouldn't get much sleep, and I wasn't wrong. The letter was weighing heavily on my mind. On one hand, I was ecstatic that he had taken the time to pour his heart out—and I didn't doubt that he meant what he'd written—but I wasn't willing to let my guard down just yet. I had a big heart and still loved him, but I couldn't forget how he had hit me or turned his back on me when I needed him most. I know my Mom would want me to welcome him with open arms and pick up where we'd left off before she died, but I wasn't sure I could do that. Not yet, anyway. He would need to put in the time and effort—and then and only then I might be able to forgive him in time, but I doubted I could ever forget.

I must have fallen asleep at some point, because I was woken up with a big, slobbery kiss from Sydney. She sure had a way about her that made me feel loved. As I got my bearings, I thought about the letter once again, and tried to figure out my feelings. I would describe my mood as guarded, at best. My time alone did nothing for me but confuse me even more. Not only did I doubt my Dad, but I doubted myself. Was I being too harsh? Was this the olive branch I so desperately had been praying for? Was he being sincere or setting me up for more heartache? So many unanswered questions left me in a funk.

CHAPTER 38

JONATHAN

As I showered and dressed for school, Luke had been busy in the kitchen making me a feast. He welcomed me with a punch on the shoulder and a big, toothy smile. "How's it going, kid?" he inquired. "I know I said I would let you be, and I will, but, and I speak from experience, it helps to talk things through. I was a lot like you at your age, and keeping issues bottled up doesn't do anyone any good." I knew he was right, but, quite honestly, I knew that if I started talking about the letter, it would open the proverbial can of worms, and I would be late for school—plus the fact that I would cry. I was on the verge just thinking about it, and I, for some reason, didn't want Luke to see me that way. I was hoping he saw me in more of a tough-guy persona with his shit together rather than a blubbery little baby. Instead of opening up, I told him "Thank you" for being my friend and that I appreciated him. Then I dug in to the fluffiest, most delicious buckwheat pancakes smothered in home-grown maple syrup.

I turned down his offer for a ride to school. It was brutally cold out, but I always thought better when I was outside and walking. It cleared my head and helped me put things into perspective. By the time I reached school, the first bell was ringing, and I felt better. My plan was to talk to Luke the first chance I got, so he could give me his perspective from an alcoholic's point of view. He had a plethora of knowledge about life in general but, most importantly, specifically about alcoholism, and I needed to pick his brain. He also didn't sugarcoat things and was in touch with his feminine side when it came to emotions. This would come in handy while he helped interpret the letter. I wondered what he would think if he could tap into my thoughts right now. This made me chuckle, and the first smile of the day washed over my face.

School was boring, as usual. Nobody questioned my absence from the day before, and I offered no explanation. My favorite subject is a toss-up between history and science. I found them both very fascinating. It wasn't hard to figure out that math was my least favorite. I failed to see how the Pythagorean theorem was going to come in useful in my everyday life, but I guess stranger things have happened. I went through the paces so I wouldn't draw unwanted attention, and, before I knew it, school was dismissed, and I was once again headed over to Luke's.

As I approached Luke's property, Sydney was there to greet me once again. Her ear-piercing squeals of joy and tail wags were the best medicine anyone could ask for, and my mood miraculously was lifted to one of optimism and contentment. Luke was inside this time, slaving over a hot stove. As usual, there was a crackling fire roaring, and the place smelt indescribably delectable. It struck me as odd and sad that I felt more at home here than at my own house, where I had lived my whole life. As Luke saw me, his eyes twinkled, and he stopped what he was doing to come over and give me a hug. It wasn't his normal great-big bear hug, but it was still pretty close to perfect.

"You know, this place seems lonely and empty when you're not here" he said. "It's like we've known each other forever." He continued as he sat down next to me with a heaping plate of gooey chocolaty goodness.

"I agree 100% with you, and I'm so glad you've come into my life because I have something to discuss with you," I replied.

With trepidation in my voice, I just dove in and spilled everything about the letter and my Dad's present state. One of the greatest things about Luke—and, trust me—there was plenty—was his ability to listen intently without interruption. I got through the whole scenario without one tear and considered this a major feat. I found myself breathing a sigh of relief after it was out in the open, and I was glad I had given myself the time to work it through in my mind in advance. The next hour or so, we spent dissecting the letter. Luke felt that my Dad was genuine but also felt that going it alone was a recipe for disaster. Addictions, he explained, were tricky, and they needed support and guidance to overcome them. To my knowledge, my Dad had neither one of these things at his disposal. As Luke talked about his addiction in relation to my Dad's, it made perfect sense. My Dad either needed a facility or, at the very least, a doctor's supervision. This worried me because I knew my Dad's wishes were to do this alone, and I was afraid that, if I tried to interfere, he would backtrack on any progress he had made or, even worse, shun the whole idea. Then we'd be back to square one.

We both sat deep in thought, trying to come up with a plan, when Luke offered, "You know what, Jonathan? I'm going to offer to be your Dad's sponsor. I hope you don't think I was overstepping, but, today, while you were at school, I drove over to your house and dropped literature about AA on your doorstep." I assured him I most definitely didn't mind, and I was thrilled he'd made such a kind gesture. We agreed to come back to this subject later. The sun had set, and we busied ourselves in the kitchen, whipping up a fiesta. We made a great team in the kitchen. He fried meat, while I grated cheese and chopped tomatoes. It was a meal fit for a king, with tacos, nachos and guacamole, followed by crunchy deep-fried churros for dessert. With our tummies full and satisfied, we threw on layers of clothes and got all our supplies ready for the box excavation. When Luke picked up the box cutters and crowbar, he also picked up some night-vision goggles and more film for the camera. We needed to be prepared for anything and everything.

CHAPTER 39

JONATHAN

If I said I wasn't nervous and a little anxious, my nose would have grown at least two inches, because I had a whole stomach full of butterflies. The unknown was a scary thing. Luke and I had discussed what we thought was in the box, and we'd come to the conclusion that it was anybody's guess. Someone had gone to great lengths to hide it, so the one thing I was sure of was that it was bad. Real, real bad. I had a sneaking suspicion that this might be what we needed to crack this case wide open—but I was reluctant in more ways than one for it to get solved. With all certainty, I wanted to get justice and closure for the poor women who'd been killed, but I also knew that, once it was over, I would have to go back to my boring, mundane life. I loved the intrigue, mystery and danger, not to mention the sneaking out at night. It made me feel kinda like a bad boy, defying the rules. I also wasn't sure where it would leave my relationship with Luke. I had grown quite fond of him and not only wanted him in my life but needed him.

The moon was hiding behind clouds tonight, and I could feel precipitation in the air. I said a little prayer that the rain would hold off until we made it out in the morning. Even though we were mostly covered by trees in there, the rain always found its way in and created the sloppiest mess. With the box in a clearing, that would create even worse conditions. Once again, Luke led the way, with Sydney and me following close behind. We remained quiet, with our lanterns off, until we were sure we were alone. The night before last had caught us off guard, and we were not about to let that happen again. As we approached the campfire spot, it appeared that we were alone. There were no burning embers or heat coming from the pit. We strapped on our miner's hats, adjusted our night-vision goggles, and got busy digging. The mound of dirt was exactly as we had left it, which eased some of my anxiety. As we reached the box, we both stopped, looked at each other and, in hushed tones, wished each other luck. A quick thumbs-up, and we began hoisting it up and out of its home. It wasn't quite as heavy as I remembered it being, but, then again, the chain had been removed. It was a hard-steel red, shiny box about 24 x 24 x 24 and, by my estimation, weighed anywhere between 100 and 125 pounds.

The moment of truth had arrived as Luke used the bolt cutters to cut through the padlock. I realized I was holding my breath and not moving a muscle. I could hear my heartbeat fast and hard in my ears as sweat dripped down my back. My stomach did a couple of flips, and, as soon as Luke opened the box, my eyes almost popped out of my head. I let out a gasp that could be heard around the globe. I turned my back and retched uncontrollably.

CHAPTER 40

JONATHAN

I was hoping that my eyes were deceiving me, but as soon as I got control of myself, I turned and took a peek inside once again—but I was not mistaken. Inside were clear boxes four deep and three high filled with a clear liquid. Floating within each one were perfectly preserved intact hands with the arm attached, up to the elbow. Every finger and nail had been preserved in its entirety. On top of each box was an assortment of different-sized plastic bags that held various and sundry things. We unpacked the boxes and noticed every hand/arm was from the left side. I wondered if this had any significance or if it was purely coincidental. In my heart, I knew that it wasn't a coincidence, but what was this madman thinking when he sawed off their limbs? Once all the boxes were removed, we noticed something lodged against the side. It was wrapped in a towel and was emitting a strong, rancid odor. I had a sneaking suspicion about what might be inside the towel, but I was hoping I was wrong. As Luke removed the towel, the leg stared back at us. It had begun to rot and shrivel up, which gave it an odd appearance. The bone was exposed in a couple of spots where the flesh and muscle had atrophied. The shoe hung haphazardly on the foot. I took a quick glance at Luke, and he looked like he had seen a ghost. Actually, seeing a ghost right then would have been a welcome distraction. We both said, "Holy crap" at the exact same time and took a moment to come to terms with this gruesome display.

The bags held everything from rings to watches and bracelets. The majority of the rings were wedding rings with sparkling diamonds. My heart ached for these poor women and their loved ones alike. Nobody deserved this kind of fate. As we were examining a box, something spooked Sydney, and she knocked one over. The arm tumbled out, and the most horrendous smell filled our nostrils. It was the unmistakable smell of formaldehyde that had been used to preserve the arms. I had my biology teacher to thank once again, since we had dissected frogs that had been soaking in formaldehyde, and I would never, ever forget that rancid smell. I was mortified that we had somehow managed to disturb the dead, as Luke brushed it off and put it gingerly back in its box. I was having a hard time fighting off the urge to vomit again. The creepiness, combined with the smell, had me at my tipping point. Some of the fingers had manicured nails, and others belonged to nail biters. A variety of tattoos adorned numerous arms and fingers. We took snapshot after snapshot for good measure. This was definitely something that needed to be documented, and we didn't want one stone to be left unturned. As much as this was making me queasy again and definitely uneasy, I knew this was the evidence we needed to go to the authorities. But first, we needed to decide what to do with them.

We contemplated burying them again, but what if the lunatic came back and moved them? All the evidence would be gone. After much deliberation, we came to the conclusion that we would take them back to Luke's and store them in his shed. The only problem was transporting them. We didn't come prepared for what we had discovered, so Luke stayed behind, much to my dismay, and I went to retrieve a wagon. I thought I had been scared before, but nothing came close to the way I felt right then. I was sickened beyond words, both physically and emotionally, and spooked by every snapping twig or scurrying rodent. Thank God Sydney came with me, or I would have been reduced to a puddle of tears.

My imagination was running wild, and I half-expected, upon my return, to find Luke dead and cut into a million pieces, but thankfully he was in one piece, standing guard over the limbs. We loaded them one by one, very carefully, so as not to jostle them too much, not forgetting the severed leg. We were careful to lower the box into the hole and cover it exactly as before, in case the lunatic returned. And then we beat feet and hightailed it out of there as fast as our legs would carry us and didn't look back. Returning back to Luke's, we unloaded our precious cargo and locked the door behind us for safe-keeping.

It wasn't until we stepped foot through the front door that we both breathed a sigh of relief. Out of all the scenarios we had considered regarding the box, not one had come remotely close to what we had discovered. I called dibs on the first shower again and couldn't get in there fast enough to try to wash off the horrors of the night. I kept playing it over and over in my mind, like it was some sick joke, but it wasn't a joke. It was real and horrendous. As I tried to picture in my mind's eye who could do something like this, I couldn't begin to fathom what kind of deranged psycho he actually was. What kind of monster were we dealing with, and were we now in more danger than before? I shuddered at the thought and blasted the hot water even more.

CHAPTER 41

JONATHAN

Skin raw from scrubbing, I sat curled up in front of the fire, drinking a cup of peppermint tea. My stomach was still doing flip-flops, and every time I thought about those boxes, I almost barfed again. My Mom had always taught me to see the good in people, but I was finding it impossible to think whoever was capable of this heinous act could have any good in them. They were evil through and through and deserved punishment equal to what they had dished out. An eye for eye was the only fitting punishment. Luke was just as disturbed as I was and kept bringing up how the limbs were just floating in the formaldehyde like they had a mind of their own.

We talked for hours, neither of us wanting to sleep for fear of what nightmares might haunt us. We watched the sun come up and heard the roosters waking up the other farm animals. I felt envious of the animals not having to deal with scum. Ignorance is bliss, so they say. I finally fell asleep out of pure exhaustion. I awoke still lying in front of the fire, while Luke was sprawled on the couch, sawing logs. His mouth was hanging open, and I had a strong urge to throw popcorn in there. This made me smile, and I was glad to see that the horror from the night before hadn't scarred me for life. I let him sleep, hoping that he was having peaceful dreams about running in a meadow somewhere with birds happily chirping while puppies and kittens frolicked in the tall grass. Life was cruel, and, no matter how hard I tried to focus on something happy and positive, my mind kept wandering back to the dreaded box with the poor, lifeless limbs.

As I peeked out the window, I saw what looked like the promise of a beautiful day. Not a cloud in the sky, but a bitter cold breeze was blowing the weather vane on top of the barn. The chickens had all taken cover in the hen house, and the horses seemed to be enjoying the cold as they ran around with not a care in the world. Since Luke was always doing everything for me, I decided it was payback time, and I raided the fridge and garden to see what snacks I could entice the horses with. As I packed my pockets with carrots, apples and other appetizing veggies, I quietly went to be one with nature.

Although it was cold and my nose was frozen, I was alive, and, for that, I was abundantly grateful. Those poor women hadn't stood a chance against the lunatic who'd been lying in wait, and this made my heart hurt. It made me all the more appreciative of what I had. Being outside was usually therapeutic to me, allowing me to clear the cobwebs out of my head and put things into perspective, but today was different. I just couldn't shake the feeling of dread. Being surrounded by death will do that to you. Images of the box nightmare lurked in every corner and brought a tear to my eye. I was a big believer in karma, and, let me tell you, this lunatic had a world of hurt coming his way. Then and only then would I be able to fully rest and begin to heal.

There's something magical about the innocence of an animal. They are just so pure and eager to please, with no judgment. It amazed me how dogs would still wag their tails after being abused. I would see those commercials on TV from animal-rescue organizations saving a mistreated animal, and they still had so much love to give. I think that's why I had so much love for animals. We were two peas in a pod.

As I approached the fence, all five horses galloped over and took turns nuzzling my neck. After I gave them carrots and apples, I was pretty sure we had become best friends for life. I was reluctant to leave the horses because their unconditional love was just what I was craving right then, but I kissed them all on their velvety snouts and promised I would return tomorrow. The chickens, on the other hand, were all huddled up together, and couldn't have cared less that I'd brought some veggies from the garden. I left it for them and figured they were just playing hard to get. I had no doubt that I could win them over. They'd be pecking at each other to get close to me in no time at all.

It was no surprise that, when I walked in the back door, Luke was cooking again. Boy, that guy loved to cook, and I was eager to eat whatever he rustled up. He inquired about how the animals were and thanked me for taking care of them, while he stirred a big dutch oven of homemade chicken noodle soup. He made a comment about chicken soup being good for the soul and how we were both in dire need of some comfort food. Never was a truer statement made. As the soup simmered, I again found my place next to the fire. There was something about a roaring fire that made me reminisce and made me miss my Mom. I wondered how my Dad was coming along and said a silent prayer that he was still on track and not suffering too badly. I would check on him tomorrow, but tonight Luke and I had a more pressing discussion to have.

CHAPTER 42

JONATHAN

We ate in silence, both lost in our own thoughts. It was delicious and really hit the spot, even though I still had a bit of a queasy tummy. Luke sensed this and got up to make me another cup of peppermint tea. I was amazed and delighted at how intuitive he was. "So, how are you doing? I can't blame you one bit for having an upset stomach. I've been dealing with the same thing on and off today," he said. He frowned as he continued, "I want to offer my deepest apologies for getting you mixed up in this. What you saw last night is what nightmares are made of, and you shouldn't have been subjected to that, especially at thirteen." It took a lot of convincing to assure him that he actually was helping me in the long run, because I would have tried to do it alone. The thought of being by myself and making that gruesome discovery was too daunting to even consider.

We retired into the family room, again by the fire, to discuss our next move. We both threw out suggestions, but the only one we agreed on was to wait it out. It was risky because we were possibly risking a young woman's life, but we both felt confident that we could catch the lunatic before he had the chance to strike once again. We basically would camp out in the forest, camouflaged, until he came and showed himself. Sooner or later, he would come to check on his "treasures"—*that* we were sure of. And when he did, we would be there. We still needed to work some kinks out as far as what we would do when that happened. Either we would stay back and take pictures or pretend like we were lost and play dumb. The playing-dumb scenario would be a little hard to pull off since, more than likely, the maniac would show his warped soul in the middle of the night. How could we realistically explain why we were casually strolling through the forest at that ungodly hour? For that reason alone, we decided that we would use this as our last resort only. We tossed around confronting him, but that was a little more than we felt equipped to handle. Bottom line was, we would just have to hurry up and wait till we were in the moment and forced to make a decision. Hopefully, we wouldn't make the wrong choice. When we went to the authorities, we needed to have him laid out on a silver platter for them to make the arrest.

We even tossed around the idea of going to the authorities with the evidence we had but vetoed that idea for a couple of reasons. The first reason was that we didn't trust them to further investigate, and then the whole thing would be for *nada*. So far, they had dropped the ball terribly, and we had no reason to think this wouldn't be the case yet again. Secondly, we didn't want them to think we were the killers, since we had possession of a lot of incriminating evidence. Our word might not be good enough, and, on the off chance there wasn't any DNA to be found, we didn't want this to backfire on us. Lastly, we both felt passionate about this and had a vested interest in seeing it through to the end.

We wanted to stay together as much as possible, so we wrote out a checklist that pretty much covered everything under the sun. The rest of the day was a whirlwind of organizing, packing and checking things off the list. Luke spent a couple of hours in the kitchen, throwing meals together and packing them into the biggest picnic basket I had ever seen. While he was cooking, I ran home real quick to check on my Dad. As I turned on my street and saw my house, it looked sad. I'm not sure how a house could actually look sad, but I could swear, if it was possible, I would have seen tears dropping from the corners of the windows. As I unlocked the door, the air fought to get out.

It too was suffocating between these walls. I walked from room to room; everything seemed in place. I opened cupboards and half-expected to see numerous gin bottles lined neatly in a row, but the cupboards only housed necessities. I ran upstairs, stopping at my Dad's door to listen, but I heard nothing. I called out but got no response. The door was unlocked, so I gathered up all the courage I could and hurried in before I changed my mind. The air was stale and smelled of sweat and barf, but the bed was neatly made. In the corner, the shrine was still in place, and a candle had been added next to the perfume. As I closed the door behind me, fear started to creep in.

Just as I started to panic, I saw a note taped to my door.

Dear Jonathan,

I hope this note finds you safe and well. I tried to kick this nasty habit alone, but I wasn't strong enough. Please don't think any less of me. I swear, I'm doing this for both of us so we can become a family again. I want more than anything to be the Dad I once was to you. I'm not delusional, and I know it will take time, but I hope you can find it in your heart to forgive me and give us another chance. Please don't worry about me. I have checked myself into a facility equipped to help me, and their success rate is good. Once again, I can't bear for you to see me like this, so I will be keeping the location a secret. I'm not sure how long I will be in. I'm sorry, from the bottom of my heart.

I love you to Pluto and back,

Dad

I breathed a sigh of relief and gave myself a moment to have a glimmer of hope. Maybe, just maybe, we could be a family again. Luke had taught me a lot about alcoholism and how it affects your actions and what you say. I'd often thought that, when my Dad was mean and hurtful, it was the alcohol talking, but it was reassuring to know I was right. I left the house feeling encouraged and ready to tackle the forest once again. The day of reckoning was quickly approaching, and it was past time to bring this deranged killer down.

CHAPTER 43

THE KILLER

There's nothing as exhilarating as the thrill of a kill. I can't explain the excitement I get when I lie in wait for the right specimen to come along. And the look in their eyes when they recognize me—even before their fate is truly realized. I just want them to understand that I'm doing them a favor and saving them from themselves before I end their feeble, miserable lives, but I'm not sure they ever fully understand. I'm not sure I fully understand myself, but yet I continue, unable to control my overwhelming urge to kill. And honestly, not wanting to. It makes me feel empowered, and I derive great satisfaction from the act of killing. It's much more rewarding than my mundane, pathetic life.

I haven't always been a beast, but I have always been an outcast. My childhood was not a happy one, to say the least. I grew up in a small town in the Midwest. We were dirt poor, but I imagine I should have been thankful that I at least had a home, since I was given up by my biological mother at birth. I was told that, for the first four months of my life, I lived in an orphanage. And then my family adopted me. That's when life should have taken a turn for the better, but, instead, I was a human punching bag. My earliest recollection from my formative years were those of pain and neglect. I was often rejected, tormented, abused, and tortured by my mother when I was allowed out of the dark closet where I spent most of my days.

Growing up, my home was a lonely one. My "mother" raised me by herself, and I had one sibling who was much older than myself. One would think that he would try to protect me, but he made himself scarce the majority of the time. As I grew up, I started out loving school, where I could escape my torturous existence at home. I was told by my teachers that I had above-average intelligence, and I enjoyed learning. What I didn't enjoy was the bullying from my fellow students. They often made fun of the fact that I was adopted, needling that even my real mom couldn't stand me. I developed a stutter, which only made them taunt me even more. It got so bad that I started harboring secret aggressive fantasies. It went from bad to worse.

As I was repeatedly ridiculed at school and abused at home, I began manifesting strange habits. I often woke up in soaking-wet sheets with a puddle of pee under my bed that I didn't even remember doing. I started experimenting with fire. The flame and heat were intoxicating to me, and I couldn't get enough. I would often go out back, fighting my way through weeds, and light whatever I could find on fire, just because I could. I had no one to talk to, so as time went on, I withdrew into my shell, living vicariously through my fantasies until I was old enough to carry them out. I'm not even sure I developed any sense of right and wrong, with no role model to teach me about trust, basic rules or about how to interact with other human beings. And no role model to learn empathy from. I turned into a calloused shell of a child, harboring horrible thoughts and enjoying every single, solitary one of them.

I muddled through my childhood angry, but, as a teenager, I learned I didn't need that life and dreamt about the time I'd be able to be on my own. I developed skills, and I was crafty with my hands, which allowed me to get paid for odd jobs around town. I stashed everything away in hopes for a brighter future. When I turned sixteen, I'd had enough; I packed up my meager belongings, with my pockets full of cash, and headed out west. I was eager to put the past behind me and start fresh in a new state with new goals, and I never looked back. Unfortunately, my past followed me, and I was unable to stop the fantasies, nor did I want to. I found my fantasies fascinating, and, as time went on, it became harder and harder to keep them contained within my brain.

I was a decent-looking young man and was able to blend into my environment. I finished school and enrolled in community college, where I majored in psychology, mainly to try to figure myself out. I was a troubled adult at this point, which all stemmed back to my lack of nurturing as an infant and toddler. What I found the craziest is that no one would have been able to tell from my physical appearance that I was damaged goods. I got a good job and hid in plain sight within my community, dating here and there but preferring my time alone so that I could visualize the heinous acts that were eating away at my soul.

As time went on, I started experimenting on animals. The immense pleasure I felt when ripping an animal apart and watching them squirm before I dismembered them was nothing short of jubilation. I ached to kill. The older I got, the more creatively my mind worked. My fantasies at this time involved women. Not just any women, but women who were married and of child-bearing age. I felt an intense desire to eliminate them, one by one, so they could not do to their children what had been done to me. Some may call this irrational, but, to me, it was who I was.

I moved around quite a bit, not fully able to find my groove until I settled in a quaint quiet town in the Pacific Northwest named Mount Sierra. There was a multitude of reasons I chose this town to plant roots in, but two main ones stuck out more than others. There was a forest that was plush and secluded that ran adjacent to the town. I felt comfortable there with the trees enveloping me in silence and muffling the sounds of the outside. It would serve as perfect grounds to bring my chosen women to their day of reckoning. The other reason was the women. The town consisted largely of young couples just starting their families. I couldn't let that happen.

There was so much rage and hostility in me toward these women that I needed to make them pay.

I would not let them reproduce and abuse their children, as I had been. And that is how it all started. Now that I'd found a place to call home, I worked myself up the ranks in my job and became a trusted official. A perfect disguise to lure the women into a sense of trust and complacency. It was perfect, and I was brilliant.

My urges and fantasies increased to the point that they could not be ignored any longer, and, in 2014, I acted on them. This was the beginning of the end for me. I had developed what I hoped would be a foolproof plan. I was in a position that allowed me to know a great many people in the community. So, to say I targeted certain women would be an accurate statement. I selected the women who fit my criteria and approached them right on the outskirts of the forest as they jogged or walked by. It was a walk in the park from there, because I oozed trust and authority. They never saw it coming, and, by the time they sensed danger, I had complete control, and there was no turning back. There was just something about that first kill that made me want more. I just didn't want it—I *craved* it deep in my warped soul.

After my first kill, I developed an MO. It wasn't intentional or planned in advance, but it just seemed like the thing to do, and it became my signature. I would disrobe the women after they had taken their last breath, fold their clothes in a neat pile and bury them in a box under the shade of a huge pine tree. It served as a burial and an end to a miserable existence. I also decided on a souvenir, so I chopped off their left arm for no other reason than that it had their wedding ring and signified their marriage and therefore the natural progression to having children. I saved them in formaldehyde to admire later. It was a convoluted thought process, but it's how my mind worked and made perfect sense to me. The joy I derived from this mutilation was euphoric, and I lived and breathed for the next victim to cross my path. Days ticked by, and my desire to kill increased. I wanted to continue to fly under the radar, so I spaced my killings out, all the while intensely craving the gleeful feeling I got while ending the life of one of those despicable women. I took great pains in cleaning up my crime scene. A ribbon here or AirPod there were sporadically placed, just to keep the hunt going, although I didn't want to get caught. Getting caught would mean allowing more women to abuse their children, and I knew I was the chosen one to make sure that didn't happen. Unfortunately, I got cocky and careless the other night.

I was cleaning up when I got spooked. I could have sworn I was being watched and heard voices. Not knowing if they were real or in my head, I fled, leaving behind a severed leg.

I had been stressing over this for days until I returned to the crime scene by the campfire and found it still lying there. Wrapping it tightly in a towel and securely placing it in the box with the limbs gave me hope. Relief washed over me, giving me unfounded confidence that this was not the end of my reign. Getting caught and convicted was a fate worse than death for me, since my only joy in life revolved around the killings. Dreaming and fantasizing about the next victim gave me life.

CHAPTER 44

JONATHAN

Neither one of us were eager to go back in, but we took the plunge and told ourselves there was light at the end of the proverbial tunnel. We'd brought the wagon along to help carry the vast amount of supplies. We weren't entirely sure how long we would be camping out, but Luke had taken this seriously and prepared for the long haul. He even remembered to make arrangements for the farm animals, just in case. Trying to be incognito proved to be more challenging than expected, but, where there's a will, there's a way, and we found the coziest spot.

Even though I had been in the forest too many times to count, it still found ways to freak me out. Don't get me wrong—there was something about the darkness and quietness that was relaxing, but, more times than not, it made me apprehensive. I always felt like eyes were following my every move and something or someone was on the verge of jumping out and scaring the crap out of me. Now that I knew there was a lunatic running free, I was more anxious than ever. Luke and I had made a pact that we would stay together, but I was convinced he'd agreed to this just to help put me at ease, but, truthfully, this wasn't the time to question him, and I welcomed it and agreed wholeheartedly.

Setting up "camp" proved to be a bit of a challenge, but we were both pleased with what we had accomplished. Now, with only time on our hands, we were both too tense to do anything but pace back and forth. We tried to play cards, but we were afraid the lantern might draw attention to us even though we had placed a camouflage tarp over our tent. We didn't dare tell ghost stories, or I would for sure chicken out and call the whole thing off. Luke started digging around in our supplies and handed me the most delectable ham sandwich I had ever had. I don't know how he did it, but everything he made was delicious. He must be some kind of culinary genius, or maybe it was because he made it with love, just like my Mom did with her one-of-a-kind sugar cookies. Whatever it was, I was hooked.

We had decided that we would take turns being on watch while the other slept—or at least tried to. Luke took the first shift, since I hadn't slept but a wink, and I was starting to drag as the adrenaline wore off. Luke had worked miracles in the tent, and it actually looked more like someone's bedroom than a tent in the middle of the forest. My sleeping bag was placed on a cot with a down pillow sprayed with lavender essential oil to relax me, and in the corner sat a table with a vase of flowers from his garden. *Seriously, what doesn't this man think of?* I couldn't help but smile and feel the love.

I didn't think there was any way that I would fall asleep, but I did, almost the second my head hit that fluffy cloud of a pillow. Not only did I fall asleep in record time, but I slept better than I slept in my own bed with the rainbow walls surrounding me. Whether it was because I was exhausted, relieved my Dad had gotten help, or the lavender-scented comfy pillow, it was a much welcome change. I was dreaming of camping with my family at the lake. I had just jumped into the lake, and it was so warm against my face. My Mom was tapping me on the shoulder, trying to get my attention, when my eyes flew open. I jumped out of my skin, not realizing where I was, until I saw Sydney sitting there with her tongue hanging out and Luke with his hand on my arm. "Wow, you were out like a light. Sydney was licking your face, and I tapped you on the shoulder for a solid minute. You were starting to scare me until I heard you call out to your Mom in your sleep. I'm sorry I disturbed you, but I figured you'd want to know that it's 9 a.m. and time for breakfast," Luke said.

I don't know how he did it, but somehow he had managed to scramble eggs and fry sausage while in the middle of the forest. I was famished. He described how his night had gone, and, thankfully, it had been tedious and uneventful. After the other night and the limb discovery, I welcomed a little peace and quiet. Luke retired into the tent for some shut-eye, and I started my watch. Sydney went with Luke, since she'd kept watch all night with him. Dogs had an incredibly keen sense of smell and supersonic hearing, so we both agreed it was best if she was on the night watch. For some reason, we had it in our mind that when the lunatic did make an appearance, it would be at night, but we weren't sure enough about that to drop our guard in the daylight hours just on the off chance. It was actually anyone's call because, clearly, this guy didn't think logically and had his own agenda.

I spent the better part of my morning wandering around, looking for more evidence. I was pretty sure we had enough to put this guy away forever, but it didn't hurt to look. If I found more, it would just be one more nail in his coffin. Unfortunately, I found nothing and came to the conclusion that he was using the campfire spot as his base and doing a lot of his killing in a variety of other locations within the forest. I was not willing to stray too far, though, just in case he showed up. I didn't want to be responsible for muffing up the whole stakeout. I could see through patches of the trees, and I saw the sun was shining. That never seemed to help in here, though. The forest always remained damp and cold no matter the temperature on "the outside." The afternoon passed slowly. I nibbled on trail mix and apple slices. Unfortunately, that wasn't my best choice of snacks, because apples always flooded me with family memories of our trips when we went apple picking. Then this made me miss my Mom and worry about my Dad. My thoughts started to spiral just when Luke appeared. That man had impeccable timing.

Days turned into nights, and one day was just like the other, as we remained on our stakeout.

We had a chalkboard in the tent that we used to mark off days, and we were on day thirteen. Lucky number thirteen! We stayed with our routine, and I was pleased to report that I continued to sleep like a rock, which I found surprising because we both smelled pretty ripe by now. I had added exercise to my daily boring days, more to help pass the time, but a little exercise never hurt anyone, either. I spent time visualizing catching the scum-sucker and sitting in the courtroom as the jury sentenced him to life without parole. That gave me a satisfied feeling that I couldn't equate to anything else. My thoughts wandered to my Dad. I hoped he was doing well. I looked forward to introducing him to Luke. Maybe they'd be best friends, and Luke would be at our house for cookouts. He already seemed like a second Dad to me, so this would be the icing on the cake for them to get along. I knew with certainty that Luke, Sydney and Buffy would remain in my life indefinitely no matter how my Dad felt, but the thought of one big happy family sounded glorious. I missed this more than I ever wanted to admit, even to myself.

And then came the subject of school. Eventually I was going to have to go back and face the music. I had a lot of absences to explain, but I was pretty sure being instrumental in the takedown of the Mount Sierra killer would qualify as a valid reason for all my time away. I knew that I had missed quite a lot, but I also knew I could play catch-up super-fast. Luckily, I had inherited my Mom's and Dad's smart genes, and school came easy to me. I took great pride in my intelligence and pretty much aced all my tests at school. Since all I've had is time to think lately, I've decided I want to follow in my Dad's footsteps and be an attorney, too. I visualized myself in the courtroom bringing justice to those who deserved it and punishment to the warped souls of the world. I imagined it would feel good to help people, and I was all about feeling good. And helping, for that matter.

If possible, Luke and I grew closer and closer as days went by. He was my rock and could read my moods better than me. We talked about everything under the sun, including my dreams and ambitions. He encouraged me to pursue my dream and promised he'd be by my side every step of the way. He even offered to pay for my college, which I found above and beyond, but I was touched and thankful all the same. I grew to have the utmost respect for him. My Mom would have liked him, and I was pretty positive my Dad would, too. To no surprise, Luke had done a phenomenal job at packing supplies and predicting how much we would need. He even remembered to bring along a radio, so we would know if the world came to an end as we lived off the grid. We were pleased to hear that there was no news of the killer striking again while we were on our stakeout. If we had anything to do with it, Alexa would be the last victim ever.

And then it happened. The day we had planned for in great detail. The day that would change our lives forever.

CHAPTER 45

JONATHAN

We had just finished our dinner and were playing Truth or Dare, yet again, when we heard footsteps. We froze and exchanged a look that said, "Here we go!" The footsteps weren't light, so we knew it had to be someone that weighed a significant amount. They were whistling and dragging something behind them. Out of nowhere the smell of a cigar filled the air. It was the same smell of French toast and cedar from the other night. That smell was ingrained in my memory from my childhood, so I was positive it was the same person. We both put on our night-vision goggles and waited till they came into clear view. It was a man, but he had his back turned to us. He was wearing what looked like a campaign hat with a broad brim. He walked straight to the

183

campfire and threw in some pine needles and a couple of logs before lighting it. It was hard to tell what he had drug behind him, but it resembled some type of animal. He deposited it next to the fire and sat down as he inhaled his cigar.

He was in no hurry to do much of anything except smoke cigar after cigar as he warmed himself by the fire. He looked like he was deep in thought—maybe scheming on ideas for his next victim. It wasn't entirely fair to make that assumption because we weren't positive he was the killer. Being in the wrong place at the wrong time didn't necessarily make one guilty of murder, although the coincidence was one I could not ignore. I thought back to what seemed like decades ago, when I stumbled upon Luke staring down at the severed leg and automatically assumed the worst. Unfortunately, people did that, and I told myself that, from here on out, I would be better than that. What was the old saying . . . you can't judge a book by its cover? But then I thought to myself, why hang out in a scary forest by yourself, unless you were up to no good—even though I had done it? Numerous times, in fact. Was it possible that this hat-wearing, cigar-smoking stranger just happened to wander to this hidden spot just for some down-time and to think? It was possible, but I knew in my gut he was up to no good. Another important thing I had learned from Luke was *always trust your gut.* My mind was racing and could convince me of anything under these circumstances.

Luke and I looked at each other; he looked so funny in those goggles I had to stifle a giggle. He smiled and put his finger over his mouth to *shhhh* me. I wondered what he was thinking. Trust me, my mind was thinking the worst again, and it was throwing a whole bunch of different scenarios out there for me to contemplate and freak out over. I took some deep breaths to calm myself. Luckily, it worked. I needed to reel myself in and concentrate on the subject at hand. Things could start moving quickly and dangerously at any second, and I needed to be focused on the present. As I took another glance at Luke, he looked focused but also cool and collected, which helped me regain my composure. Always helpful—even when he wasn't even trying!

The man reached behind his back and pulled out a huge knife. I put my hand over my mouth to stifle the scream that was on the verge of escaping. He leaned over, grabbed the animal off the ground, and, in one swift movement, he sliced a hind leg off. He acted with such precision that clearly said this was not his first time mutilating something or someone. The knife had to be incredibly sharp to cut through bone without any difficulty, and my mind went places that made me cringe. There was something about the way he moved that was alarming. He seemed sure of himself, like he was untouchable and above the law. As he held up the leg, blood dripped all over his hand and pooled on the ground. He brought his hand to his mouth and licked each finger, sucking the blood and savoring every drop. This grossed me out to the max and made me dry-heave.

We continued to watch, puzzled yet fascinated and mildly repulsed, as he ripped the animal to shreds like a wild beast.

He then commenced cooking the raw meat over the fire with a broken tree branch as a spit. I was relieved when the smell of pork wafted through the air. I had been so scared that he had killed someone's beloved dog with his bare hands and dragged it into the forest to devour like a caveman. After he'd eaten, he once again licked his fingers and wiped his mouth clean with his sleeve. We both were eager for him to make a move and show us his identity, but we waited patiently. Our efforts paid off when he got up, stretched and turned to face us as he stoked the fire. He was a man about 55 and looked familiar, but where did I know him from? He was wearing jeans, cowboy boots and a thick winter coat. I was racking my brain, trying to figure out why he was so familiar looking.

And then it came to me. I remembered. I had seen his picture in many newspaper articles and heard him speak on the news. I couldn't believe who I was looking at, but this put everything in a brand-new light and explained a whole lot.

CHAPTER 46

JONATHAN

Staring me in the face was none other than Dan Osborne, sheriff of Mount Sierra. He was bigger in person than I imagined. As this sunk in, I looked at Luke, and he raised his eyebrows and mouthed *Oh, my goodness.* He recognized him as well. As we gave the magnitude of our discovery a second to sink in, Mr. Osborne was on the move, heading straight for the tree where the box lay empty. Ahead of time, Luke and I had decided that our plans would unfold depending on who showed up. If we felt we could overpower them without getting harmed, we would. If not, we would hang back and take as many pictures as we could. The pictures were an iffy scenario because of the darkness and shadows. We would have to move quickly, with one of us shining the flashlight at our culprit at the exact time they were looking at us so the other could snap the picture. Too many factors to screw up, and then we would have blown our chance and shown our hand. This was not the plan of choice, and now being privy to the fact that it was the sheriff and that, likely, he was armed, this could lead to a deadly scenario. One which neither Luke nor I wanted any part of.

This added a whole 'nother element to the already-scary situation. Just as I had suspected, Luke had brought along a gun—he'd confided in me during our game of Truth or Dare one night. I voiced my opinion on guns loud and clear, but he assured me it was only for protection. It could be a matter of life and death, and, even though I despised guns, his explanation made me realize the importance of this situation, and I was thankful that he'd had the foresight to pack it with our supplies. Once again, for the billionth time, I appreciated him having my back.

I was still trying to come to terms with the fact that the sheriff of our quaint little town was a cold-blooded killer. And not just any killer but a *serial* killer with an intentional motive. It sickened me that he had betrayed the trust of the town and spat in their faces in the worst possible way. It explained why the cases had gone unsolved. Actually, it explained a whole lot. It gave him the opportunity to gain the trust of these poor women, who then fell victim to his game, and, in turn, he could abuse the system to cover his tracks. He had been rigging the system for more than five years and had the audacity to prey on the poor women whom he had vowed to protect. It was the worst possible betrayal, and I found it not only repulsive but unforgivable and completely unfathomable.

Luke leaned over and whispered in my ear to give him a thumbs-up if I agreed we should go with our first plan. It would involve using force and probably the gun, but I agreed that the stakes were too high to risk letting the sheriff escape, only to kill again. I gave him the thumbs-up and was left standing alone while he rummaged around for the gun in our tent and the sheriff disappeared behind a tree. Luke returned at exactly the same time the sheriff came out from behind the tree with a couple of shovels. He commenced to digging, while we stood in silence, about to pounce the second he realized the box was empty. The tension in the air was beyond belief. I had been scared more in the past couple of weeks than in my whole time alive, and I was looking forward to chilling for a while when this was all said and done. A trip to the Pacific Ocean just to listen to the waves splash against the shore with Sydney by my side sounded just like something the doctor would order to get my mind in the right place and to heal from this nightmare. I didn't anticipate the downtime to last long, though, because I knew myself well enough to know that I craved danger and excitement. Another trait Luke and I shared which made me positive that adventure would come knocking on our door once again for us to explore.

The suspense was killing us. We watched him dig a couple of shovels of dirt and then take a break. He was in no hurry—that was for sure. Although I was scared, I was equally as excited that we were going to bring justice to the poor women as well as their families. I knew that, once the sheriff opened the box, things would move fast and furious. We would have to work with precision to bring him down. Luke once again whispered in my ear that he was proud of me and under no circumstances was I to take a chance of any type. He was afraid shots could get fired, and, if that started happening, I was told to immediately abort the mission and seek shelter. He added that he would never forgive himself if something were to happen to me and gave me a quick hug.

Waiting proved to be insufferable. I wanted to go ask him if he needed some help, he was moving so slow! A couple shovels full of dirt at a time made for some slow progress, but we stood waiting and watching with bated breath—and then waiting some more. I figured that about an hour had passed and that he must be getting close. The mound of dirt was fairly large by now, and the moment of truth was upon us. He set his shovel down, wiped the sweat from his brow and started fishing around in his pocket. He pulled out a key ring with a whole bunch of keys attached. He fidgeted with those for a while and then set them on top of the mound of dirt. He disappeared behind the trees for a second time and came back with some straps to help him hoist the box out of the hole. Once those were attached, he began raising the box out of the hole. Just as we anticipated, he would grow suspicious once the box proved lighter than it should be. He stopped, removed his hat and scratched his head. I felt like I could see the wheels moving inside his head as things began to click into place. We held our breath and moved ever so slowly, trying not to make a peep until we were within ten feet of him, but still hidden.

After giving it a moment's thought, he continued to raise the box ever so slowly. He wasn't in any hurry with anything, and I prayed that he was just savoring the moment, very unlike his quick actions when he killed the women. The thought of them suffering was too much to comprehend. The box was visible; he grabbed his keys to unlock the padlock—and he noticed that it was no longer there. He removed his hat once again, let out an audible sigh, looked around in confusion and inspected the box from every angle. To say he looked perplexed would have been an understatement. As he opened the box, we pounced. We knew we had to catch him off guard, or else he would be on high alert and grab his gun. We needed to gain the upper hand. While Luke shouted, "Stop right there, sheriff, and put your hands where I can see them," I turned on the lanterns and started feverishly taking pictures. It all happened so fast I didn't have time to think. I saw the look of surprise on the sheriff's face, and, at that instant, I knew he was not going down without a fight.

Next thing I knew, the sheriff drew his gun and took a swing at Luke. They ended up on the ground, wrestling each other for control of the gun. I picked up a shovel and tried to hit the sheriff over the head, but I couldn't get a clean shot. The sheriff was yelling obscenities, and Luke was telling him to give up and turn himself in. Dirt and pine needles were flying everywhere, and then, with the loudest boom, a bullet ricocheted off a nearby tree. I was yelling for Luke to be careful just as I heard another shot fired. This time, I knew it had made contact with someone because one of them screamed out in agony. My stomach dropped to my feet, and I felt weak in my knees, like I could pass out. I must have started hallucinating, because I could swear I heard someone yelling my name. Over and over again, frantically calling *Jonathan, Jonathan—where are you?*

I ran over to the two men not knowing what I would find. The sheriff was still yelling obscenities at Luke as Luke rolled over, grabbing his side in pain. Blood was everywhere, and I didn't know what to do. Luke looked at me with pain in his eyes and passed out. I was torn between helping Luke and trying, somehow, to stop the sheriff. Luke and I had not planned for this scenario, so I needed to think fast, but before I even had a chance, the sheriff jumped up and pointed the gun at me. It's true what they say—my life actually flashed before my eyes, and I just knew I was about to share the same fate as the women victims. I closed my eyes and said a silent prayer as he grabbed me and shoved the gun in my back. I just kept thinking about how I would never see my Dad again and that Luke would be so disappointed that we didn't get the justice we'd worked so hard for. The only positive was that I would see my Mom again.

CHAPTER 47

JONATHAN

I don't know why I didn't think of this before, but Sydney would gladly come to my rescue. Luke had closed her up in the tent so she wouldn't be in danger or get in the way. If I could somehow get to her, she could help. I just knew it. Just when I started yelling for her, I heard someone screaming my name at the same time Sydney was barking up a storm. The sheriff looked flustered and out of sorts. With a quaver in his voice, he gained control and told me to shut up and move or he would shoot. I didn't feel like tempting fate, so I moved. He was leading me away from the campfire, deep into the forest. I glanced over my shoulder and saw Luke sprawled out on the ground, seemingly lifeless. This lit a fire under me I had never experienced before. I turned on my heel and punched the sheriff square in the jaw and then kneed him in the crotch as I caught him off guard. He went down reeling in pain, and I ran like I have never run before, straight to the tent to let Sydney out. She was barking and scratching to get out and greeted me with a lick. "Come on, girl. Luke is hurt, and we're in danger, so we have to run for help and fast." I wasn't sure that she understood, but I like to think dogs are smarter than people give them credit for and can sense danger and moods. I knew she could feel my energy and took off running by my side.

I took a quick look over my shoulder to see if I was being followed, but I was alone, at least for the time being. I knew it would be only a matter of minutes before the sheriff caught up to me. I ran in the opposite direction he had been leading me, in hopes that this would buy me some time.

And ran straight into my Dad, accompanied by a slew of deputy sheriffs.

I had never been so happy to see anyone in my whole life. "Dad, what are you doing here? How did you know where I was? When did you get out?" I inquired. I didn't even wait for him to answer before I started rambling non-stop about what had happened and that we needed to move fast or the sheriff would get away—not to mention the medical attention Luke needed ASAP.

Sydney and I took off toward the campfire while the others followed close behind. Luckily I hadn't made it very far, so when we reached our destination, the sheriff was just getting up and dusting himself off. I let the deputies take over from there and ran to check on Luke. He was white as a sheet and lying so still, I thought he had passed. I immediately burst into tears and laid my head on his chest. I was sobbing for him not to leave me as my Dad looked on.

Confusion clouded his eyes. That's when I heard a shallow groan emerge from deep within Luke's soul. I put my hand on his neck and could feel his heart beating very slowly and irregularly. I knew he wasn't going to make it if we didn't act quickly. The next minutes were a complete blur as everyone kicked into overdrive. Before I knew it, help had arrived, and Luke was being loaded onto a stretcher. I refused to leave his side, so my Dad stayed with me offering support, still looking as confused as ever. Sydney didn't understand and hung her head and whimpered.

I watched with extreme satisfaction as the sheriff was handcuffed and led away. He glared at me, yelling that I was going to be sorry I ever messed with him and then spit in my direction. My only regret at that moment was that Luke wasn't coherent enough to witness this all going down the way we had hoped. Needless to say, I didn't have a lot of faith in the sheriff's department, which led to my desire to stay behind and protect the evidence, but I took a leap of faith and let them do their work. What are the chances they were *all* corrupt, anyway? I knew my place was with Luke. He needed me and all the good, positive juju I could muster up if he was going to make it. As Sydney, my Dad and I walked away from the campfire, I took one last look over my shoulder, and all I saw was a sea of yellow caution tape among a big, red blood-soaked spot where Luke had been lying.

CHAPTER 48

JONATHAN

After I begged to go with Luke in the ambulance, the paramedics reluctantly agreed to let me ride with him—only after my Dad convinced them they had his blessing and that it was the right thing to do for everyone involved. I had never appreciated my Dad more than at that moment. I knew he had so many questions, but he had put my needs first. At long last. I patted Sydney on the head and gave her a big hug, trying to reassure her everything would be alright and that we would all be reunited soon. She offered me her paw and one of her infamous kisses. She seemed to understand and sat obediently by my Dad's side.

As we sped away, my head was swimming with unanswered questions as the sirens pierced through my ears. I held

Luke's hand, kissed him gently on the cheek and whispered in his ear that I loved him. I was trying to be strong for his sake, but I was falling short of accomplishing that. I began to cry. "Luke, I need you. You and I make the best team—you can't leave me. Please fight for us and Sydney, because my life won't be complete without you in it." As I looked into his face, his eye opened, and he breathlessly whispered, "I love you, Jonathan. I'm so proud of you, son." And then, just like that, he was gone. I sat mortified and heartbroken, begging the paramedics not to let him die. They worked feverishly as I looked on in utter shock and dismay as the ambulance pulled up in front of the emergency entrance. The last image I have in my mind is my friend, Luke, the gentle giant, lying unresponsive and lifeless as they wheeled him through the door.

As I stood outside the door, I was crying so hard I couldn't catch my breath. How is it possible that this wonderful man with the heart of pure gold could be gone? It seemed like I had known him forever, with all the impact he had made in my life. He was the best thing that ever happened to me, showing me unconditional love and teaching me to believe in myself. No one had been able to help me come to terms with my Mom's death and to look to the future with optimism like he had. I was just getting ready to walk into the emergency room when my Dad and Sydney pulled up in a sheriff's cruiser. I ran into my Dad's arms, hysterical. Sydney came and nuzzled me, trying to tell me everything would be all right. But she was wrong. Nothing would ever be the same again. Not without my inspiration and best friend.

My Dad had me sit tight with Sydney as he went inside to see if he could get any information for me, but, unfortunately, he was told nothing, because he wasn't related. I couldn't even think straight at this point. All the talks Luke and I had had in the past were flooding my mind. The thoughtfulness and protectiveness he showed me was more than anyone could ever imagine, let alone experience. For it to be gone was more than I could fathom. I refused to leave and sat huddled in a ball, sobbing my eyes out, while Sydney nuzzled my neck and licked my tears.

CHAPTER 49

JONATHAN

Just as my Dad was going to explain how he knew I was in the forest, the paramedics walked through the door. I jumped up and almost tackled them, begging for information. I tried so hard to read the expression on their faces, but they remained stoic. *Tools of the trade*, I imagined. I knew I was going to be happier than I had ever been or be destroyed by what they said next. The suspense was killing me as they walked me over to a bench and sat down.

The words they said next will forever be emblazoned in my soul. "Son, we're not supposed to divulge information like this and could get in big trouble, but we saw and felt the bond you had with that gentleman, so we feel compelled to put your mind at ease. The ER doctors were able to revive your friend, but he is far from out of the woods (*No pun intended*, I thought) yet. He is in very critical condition, and, if by the grace of God he recovers, he will have an uphill battle."

I almost peed myself with excitement. I yelled *"Yippee!"* and jumped around like a little kid on Christmas morning who'd just got a new puppy. I hugged them both and told them I was eternally grateful for their quick response and being instrumental in saving Luke. My excitement must have been contagious, because it became a big giant love fest, with hugs and high fives. Sydney jumped up and down while my Dad looked on, perplexed.

I wasn't allowed to see Luke while he got settled into the ICU, but I stood outside the hospital and sent healing thoughts and positive juju his way; I made a promise I would return in the morning. My Dad hailed a cab and told him to take us home, but I refused until I checked on Luke's house and the animals. Seeing the determination in my eyes, he caved and allowed me to give the driver Luke's address instead. I owed it to Luke to make sure everything was functioning properly after all he had done for me.

As happy as I was to see my Dad looking reasonably healthy and—best of all, sober—there was some friction between us that was hard to explain. We rode in silence, neither one of us knowing what to say or how to break the ice. Since I met Luke, I have changed. I have grown and matured emotionally. I am more confident and secure in who I am and handle things with more of a level head. Trust me, I am still in touch with my feminine side and cry over sad things, but I feel more emotionally stable. All thanks to Luke's and my many heart-to-heart talks. He always told me that being an outsider looking in allowed him to get a better perspective on my situation, which, in turn, allowed him to offer logical-but-heartfelt advice and guidance. He had been my own personal therapist, and I couldn't appreciate him more.

I was never so happy to walk through the door of Luke's cabin. It felt like home, and, upon entering, I could feel the love that lived within these walls. My Dad said he felt like he was trespassing and stood at the doorway, reluctant to come in. It took a lot of convincing on my part. I finally just told him he was free to go but that I was staying. End of story, no debate. I was starting to like the new me. No more wishy-washy Jonathan but instead a determined, driven, independent young man. As my Dad stood in the entryway looking around, I invited him in to have a seat. Sydney beelined to her bed and commenced falling fast asleep on her back, with her paws in the air, happy to be home. Buffy ran down from the loft and demanded some petting as she wove in and out between my legs. Boy, it felt good to be "home"!

I offered my Dad something to drink because I knew this is what Luke would have done. He refused, but at least I succeeded in getting him to take a load off. My thoughts kept drifting to the hospital, and I was hoping things were taking a turn for the better for Luke. I spent the morning feeding and tending to the animals, among other chores. It felt good knowing I was helping Luke somehow. Whomever he had hired to take care of them had done an amazing job, but then I expected as much from Luke. He never left a stone unturned, always two steps ahead.

The animals were therapeutic, and just being around them lightened my mood and gave me the hope I desperately was craving right now. When I finished the chores, I found my Dad on the couch fast asleep, with Buffy curled in a tight ball, nestled between his legs. I let him be and went into the kitchen to make some tea.

On the kitchen table, under a vase of wilted, drooping flowers was an envelope with my name on it scrawled in Luke's hand. I stood staring at it for a couple of minutes, brushing my fingers against my name, willing Luke to live. I was excited and scared to read it—both at the same time. I made my tea and went up to the loft to be alone, just in case my Dad woke up.

My dearest Jonathan,

If you're reading this, things didn't go as planned. I'm truly sorry that our time together has come to an end. You have been a breath of fresh air to my lonely days. I have grown quite fond of you, to say the least, and think of you as the son I always wanted. Not to mention my friend. A friend I needed in the worst ways. Besides my life with Claire, you have meant more to me than I could ever put into words.

I want you to know that I have put your name on my house. I've seen you with the animals and how you light up when they're around, so I know they'll be in the best of hands. My hopes are that you can reconcile with your Dad and that you can both come live here together. I know you mentioned that your house doesn't feel like home anymore, so I hope you and your Dad can start over here. Live here, and fill the house with love, please. Sydney and Buffy love you every bit as much as they love me, so please take care of them as well.

Now, for something I've wanted desperately to tell you and have started to a million times but wasn't quite sure how. I wish I didn't feel the need to tell you, but I owe this much to you. You have the right to know. The thought of hurting you hurts me deep in my soul. Please keep in mind that this happened when I was drinking, and we all know how drinking can impair your judgment. Trust me—my judgment was deeply impaired, and if there's some way I could turn the clock back, I would, in a heartbeat, but as they say, everything happens for a reason.

Last year, before I joined AA, I was feeling lonely, deserted and worthless, so I went out drinking. Tired of the same local watering holes, I decided to try something new and went out of town. I'm embarrassed to admit I got stinking drunk and made choices I would give anything to change, but, unfortunately, there are no do-overs in life, only lessons learned. The only wise choice I made that night was not to get behind the wheel. A choice that potentially saved my life and others. But I did hitch a ride with a total stranger whom I thought was sober enough to drive my sorry ass home. I was sadly mistaken. You see, we got into an accident that night. And son, it pains me to tell you this, but it was you and your Mom who we hit. Please don't hate me. I hate myself enough for both of us and have lived with this haunting me for close to fourteen months. I can still hear you in my dreams, nightly, screaming for your Mom to wake up. To think that I am inadvertently responsible for your Mom's death, your trauma and your Dad's alcoholism wrecks me. Maybe this is karma biting me in the butt one last time. Please know that when we met, I didn't know you were the devastated kid from the accident. It wasn't until one of our heart-to-hearts when you mentioned the accident that I started putting two and two together. And, much to my dismay, after doing research, I was faced with the brutal truth.

Please—I beg of you—forgive me. I, too, was in the wrong place at the wrong time, but that doesn't make it right. I wish I could have been man enough to explain this to you before, but I was afraid of losing the best thing that's ever happened to me. I truly am sorry, Jonathan, from the bottom of my heart.

I love you, son. Have a good life. I wish nothing but the best for you, and I look forward to watching you grow up and having a family of your own. I hope you share the memory of our truly special friendship with them. Yours always and forever,

Luke

I was dumbfounded and at a loss for words. I must have reread the letter five times before I fully absorbed the impact of his confession. Part of me was angry that he was drunk and made a lame mistake by getting into a car with a drunk total stranger, while part of me was disappointed that he had kept it from me. But the biggest part of me was proud of him for confessing to something that had been eating away at him for months, when, ultimately, it wasn't his fault. To take ownership just showed what a stand-up guy he actually was. This didn't surprise me one bit, because I had known this from our first talk. I was deeply saddened that he actually thought I would hate him. I honestly couldn't think of anything that would make me hate him. Now, more than ever, he needed to pull through, so I could put his mind at ease and assure him that he wasn't getting rid of me that easily.

CHAPTER 50

JONATHAN

Thankfully, my Dad was still out like a light. I wasn't ready to share the letter just yet or explain my relationship with Luke. I was unsure how my Dad would accept the fact that Luke had filled his shoes in more ways than one. I really did love my Dad and was eager to get our relationship back on track but not to the detriment of my relationship with Luke. I was hoping that it didn't come to a place where I was forced to choose between the two. Blood was supposed to be thicker than water, but the bond I had with Luke was unbreakable. My ideal situation would be if we could all get along harmoniously, but I wasn't entirely sure this would happen. I was aware that many people would question my bond with Luke, when we hadn't known each other a lifetime, like my Dad and I obviously had, but I didn't feel like I owed anyone an explanation. It really wasn't anybody's business, and, honestly, it was hard to explain. I was kinda shocked by it myself, but it was undeniable.

The letter weighed heavily on my mind. I was not surprised in the least that Luke had made plans for all his ducks to be in a row. He was always a planner and a step ahead of the game. I was still shaken by the amount of guilt he had been carrying around. I was pretty sure my Dad and I wouldn't see eye to eye on this, so I decided not to share just yet. I hadn't yet decided if I would share, but I wanted and needed him to get to know Luke the way I knew him first. If he knew that Luke was in the car that killed my Mom, he would blame him and probably want to strangle him on the spot. Needless to say, I wasn't about to let that happen, so for the time being, this information would be a secret that only Luke and I shared.

I was beyond eager to find out how Luke was doing, but I reminded myself to put a little faith in his doctors. He was a strong, big man who had carved out a relaxing, full life for himself. He had stared demons in the eye and come out on top, so I knew he would fight with everything he had. Just as I was losing myself in memories of Luke, there was a knock at the door. As I ran to answer it, I noticed my Dad stirring while Sydney lay snoring in her bed. Two deputies stood, looking half frozen, with Luke's wagon overflowing with our supplies from the forest. With all that had been happening,

I'd forgotten all about our things. Seeing our belongings and having a faint hint of lavender filter through my nose made me misty and ache deep in my soul. I quickly wiped a lone tear from my cheek and thanked them profusely. I begged for news about Luke, but they remained tight-lipped, saying only that they would be in touch soon for a statement. As the door shut, I realized I was alone with my Dad.

He was fully awake by this point and was eager to talk. I, on the other hand, was not, but he wasn't getting the hint or taking no for an answer. So, out of respect for him, after lighting a fire, I sat and let him do all the talking. He explained in great detail the detox process in the facility. It sounded horrendous. I was proud of my Dad for sticking with the program. I'm sure there were times when he wanted to throw in the towel or tap out. He continued and explained that, with an alcoholic, the healing process was never-ending, and support was the key to success. He sounded like a parrot because I had heard the exact same words come out of Luke's mouth.

It was one thing they saw eye to eye on; now, if only they could find more common ground. I was more positive—after hearing how distraught my Dad was with his return to an empty house and me nowhere to be found—that *I* was more common ground. Maybe this would be easier than I thought!

Minutes turned into hours as my Dad outlined the next steps. He had attended his first AA meeting and was bound and determined to make amends as outlined in step #9. I never thought of my Dad as an extremely religious man, but his new sobriety had turned over a new leaf in him that I could get used to real quick. I told him that Luke, too, was an alcoholic and had offered to be his sponsor, but I could tell by the look on his face that Luke was not a subject he cared to discuss. I was feeling optimistic, though, because, if he truly was embracing the twelve-step process AA laid out, he would eventually learn to accept Luke and our relationship. I was willing to give him all the time he needed to get to that harmonious existence I was hoping for. The passion in my Dad's eyes was cause for celebration, so I pulled out some sparkling cider and offered cheers to the new-and-improved man he had become.

I had to admit I was impressed and oh-so-thankful at how he had figured out where I was.

Finally thinking coherently when he returned home to an empty house, he first called the school and then my old soccer coach before calling any remaining friends he could think of. When he hit a brick wall, he decided to look for clues around the house, which eventually led him to my computer. I had not cleared my search history, so he was able to pull up the articles I had been researching and read every single one. Knowing me and my sense of adventure, he knew I could not sit idle without investigating. He still wasn't sure where I was until he canvassed the house for clues. Finding my ripped blue jacket with pine needles still stuck in the sleeves and coming out of my pockets along with my muddy white sneakers in the mud room, he put two and two together. He was positive I was somewhere in the forest but didn't know the location. His real problem came when he tried to convince the deputy sheriffs. With no concrete evidence that a crime had been committed or that I was a missing person who potentially could be in grave danger, they were reluctant to offer assistance. He took the *Where there's a will, there's a way* approach, and, with pure determination and perseverance, he was able to convince them.

Once deep in the forest, the rest was easy since he just followed the noise and gunshot. As they say, the rest is history. I thanked my Dad for saving my life and told him I was proud of him for taking the steps in the right direction to cure his nasty addiction. His smile and the twinkle in his eyes melted my heart, and I had the first real glimmer that my Dad was back—back to being the Dad I needed and had missed so desperately. It was the moment I had dreamt about but lost sight of, because—let's face it: Things had gone from bad to worse around my house for the past fourteen months. I was confident that the healing could begin, and we would be back to being buddies once again, hopefully, with Luke along for the ride, too. We could become The Three Amigos or The Three Musketeers. I liked the way that sounded!

CHAPTER 51

MICHAEL

I was finally able to breathe a sigh of relief. I had found Jonathan. Well, and in one piece. Yet, I still feel like an outsider. Now that my treatment is behind me, I can finally think and see clearly. It's painful for me to face the damage I have caused in our relationship. Physically, I'm fine now, but, mentally, I'm damaged. I am trying my hardest to come to terms with the fact that I was physically abusive to my own flesh and blood. The one person who means more to me than life itself. AA has taught me that I must own up to my mistakes and make amends to those who suffered the brunt of my tirades. I know it must be addressed, but he will barely look at me, and, when he does, I can tell it's out of respect only. And I don't blame him. I just hope and pray that the damage I've caused is not irreversible.

I totally understand that he would turn to another for the support and love he had craved but not gotten from me, but I am jealous of his friendship with this man he calls "Luke." He idolizes him, and I can see how comfortable he is around him and in his cabin. While I have been struggling with my alcoholism, my son has moved on, so to speak. Is it too late for us? Will he be open to giving me a chance and see that I've changed, now that he has someone else to be his friend and father figure?

He keeps wanting to share stories, and I don't want to hear them. I know this is wrong, and I need to find it within myself to be supportive. I truly am thankful that Jonathan has found someone to fill the void I had created in his life, but I'm better now, so I want that person to be me. I also know I must be patient. The rift between us wasn't made overnight, so I need to give it time to heal. Time to prove I am ready and more than willing to be the Dad I once was.

I just need some time to adjust to our new normal. I need somehow to get to know this guy Jonathan adores and become friends with him, so that I can get Jonathan back. At this point, if I don't stop this petty jealousy, Jonathan will choose him over me. I can see how strongly Jonathan feels about him and the bond they share. He lights up when he talks about him, but if I have to hear how *his heart is made of pure gold* one more time, I might scream! I get it, Jonathan—he has taken over where I left off, and I need to change that. I'm slightly optimistic, though, because he did say he was proud of me for beating my addiction and thanked me for saving him. I don't blame him for being guarded and reluctant to welcome me back into his life with open arms. I need to gain that trust, and I know it will take time. I have all the time in the world to give if I know we can once again be best buddies like before, when Emma was still alive. Baby steps in the right direction are always welcome.

CHAPTER 52

JONATHAN

My Dad was eager to get home, rambling on about how he felt like an intruder in Luke's house. No matter how much I assured him this was truly nowhere near the truth, he resisted. I tried to talk about Luke and our friendship, but my Dad only half-listened and would immediately change the subject. I came to the realization that he was jealous. I was actually kind of touched that he felt this way, but only for the time being. I was willing to give him time to get used to the idea that my best friend was older than him. The sooner he came around, the better, because I wasn't about to give up my friendship with Luke or my relationship with my Dad, for that matter. With a heart as big as Luke's, I knew that, if he pulled through, he would welcome my Dad into

215

our inner circle with no qualms whatsoever. Now, we just had to get Luke better. My Dad insisted he go home, but I refused to go along with him. I needed to get our forest stuff organized and put away and go to the hospital. I could tell he was hurt and didn't understand, but he put on a brave face nonetheless, and we made plans to meet up later.

I arrived at the hospital, having decided ahead of time that I would demand answers. I couldn't rest until I found out how my friend was. With an extreme amount of trepidation, I pushed through the doors of the ICU. Luckily the nurses were too focused on their job to pay me any attention, and I blended in like I was any other family member checking on their loved one. I walked from room to room, acting like I knew what I was doing, until I saw Luke's name on a placard outside his door.

To say I was reluctant to walk through the door not knowing what I would find on the other side was an understatement. I was anxious, nauseous and on the verge of peeing my pants. I despised hospitals with a purple passion and was scared half out of my mind. Usually just driving by one made me squeamish, but here I was, in the flesh, standing outside his door. I kept reminding myself over and over that it wasn't about me and that this was for Luke. He needed my support. And lots and lots of prayers mixed with oodles of positive juju. And after everything he had done for me, if it was the last thing I did, I was not going to let him down.

My breath caught in my throat, and I felt the color drain from my face as I saw my friend lying there, unmoving, the same color as the white sheet that adorned his bed. I had to look twice, much to my dismay, to make a positive ID. There must have been a minimum of ten tubes going in and out of him connected to beeping machines. His eyes were closed, and a machine was doing the breathing for him. I cautiously walked to his bedside and gingerly took his hand in mine. He was cold and clammy. I found an extra blanket in the closet and wrapped it around him as best as I could. A tear ran down my cheek as I pleaded for him to get better. The afternoon came and went with no change as I sat by his side, holding his hand, telling him about life on the farm. I was determined to will him to live, and, if it meant me coming here, sitting day in and day out, so be it. A small price to pay to get my friend back healthy and in one piece again.

The days turned into weeks, and I kept a vigil at his bedside. I left only when I was forced to or I had to tend to the animals. Life on the farm was my therapy. I poured out my heart to the horses as they nuzzled my neck and covered me with rough, slobbery kisses. Sydney somehow understood as I explained to her in great detail what was going on with her master. I took her for long runs in the fields every day, which eased my tensions as well as tired her out. My Dad begged me to take care of myself, but it wasn't about me any longer. My Dad became so concerned about my well-being that he would come to the hospital and sit with me, willing Luke to get better. This touched me more than I told him. He was slowly coming around and would finally listen to stories about how my friendship with Luke came to be. He was finally beginning to see the man Luke was through my eyes.

Ever so slowly, I saw improvements taking place. A slight opening of an eye or move of his fingers within my hand gave me hope. It didn't take long for word to spread throughout the hospital that there was a local celebrity fighting for his life in the ICU. An article had come out on the front page of the *Pacific Sun Times*, calling us ". . . hometown heroes . . ." I waited to read it to him until I knew he could fully grasp the heroic effort it took to bring down the sheriff. The whole hospital staff was rooting for him and would stop by to wish him well and cheer him on. The deputy sheriffs had come by to get his statement numerous times, but it wasn't till week three that he had his breathing tube removed and could begin to utter a word here and there. That was the day I knew he was going to be all right and the first day I allowed myself to breathe a sigh of relief and cry tears of joy instead of sorrow. It was also the day I told him I could never hate him and forgave him for the accident. As he lay there listening, tears streamed down his face, and he grabbed my hand, planted a kiss on my fingertips and whispered, "Thank you, son. I love you."

Shortly after that, he was moved to a private room. I filled it with balloons and Get Well Soon banners. Flowers were dropped off by the dozens by well-wishers throughout the town. It was indeed a reason to celebrate. My Dad even got caught up in the joy and helped hang the banners and arrange the flowers. It was the best day I had experienced in months and long overdue. I had the two most influential men in my life under the same roof, with high hopes that they were on the right track to becoming best friends. Luke was still a far cry from healed, but the improvements he had made were nothing short of a miracle. My prayers had been answered, and I felt confident he was on his way to being back to his old, jovial self. He thanked me profusely for being by his side and willing him to live. I assured him I wouldn't have it any other way and that it was the least I could do, since he would have done the same for me.

My Dad had gone home for the night, but I stayed behind to read Luke the article from the *Pacific Sun Times*. I was proud of us. We had made a fantastic team and succeeded in bringing down the Mount Sierra killer. Something deep in my soul knew this would not be our last adventure. We both shared the need for adventure and crime-solving, no matter the danger involved. Luke finally had gotten some color back in his cheeks and was starting to look and act like his old self. As I propped pillows behind him, I asked "Are you ready for me to read you the article that put Mount Sierra on the map?" "I thought you'd never ask!" he said, with a big smile on his face and a twinkle in his eyes. Boy, was that good to see!

I not only read him the article but showed him that we had made the front page, alongside an article about the sheriff with a mugshot that showed him defeated and a little pissed. This gave us a tremendous amount of joy that I personally didn't feel the least bit of guilt about.

The article read . . .

"Gulf War Veteran and Mountain View High Freshman Single-Handedly Catch Mount Sierra Killer."

"Mount Sierra can breathe a sigh of relief as we celebrate our hometown heroes, Luke Travers, a decorated Gulf War veteran and Jonathan Elliott, a freshman at Mountain View High School, as they orchestrated the arrest of our own Sheriff Dan Osborne the night of October 13. Travers and Elliott had been unacquainted until the pair met up while individually investigating strange noises heard in the forest on the east end of the town adjacent to the Mount Sierra Campgrounds. Travers has been unavailable to interview as he recovers in the ICU from a near-fatal gunshot wound suffered in a scuffle leading up to the arrest of Sheriff Dan Osborne. Elliott explained that it all started one night about a month ago, when he heard a blood-curdling scream while walking in the forest. That prompted him to investigate, and, subsequently, he stumbled upon evidence and Travers, who was leading his own investigation. The two became instant friends, decided two heads were better than one and joined forces to bring justice to the women killed as well as their families, who have suffered. A total of twelve murders had taken place and were left unsolved due to the alleged cover-up by the Sheriff. Bail has been denied, and the sheriff remains locked up, pending his upcoming trial. A parade celebrating the two is being planned the first weekend in December upon Travers' recovery. Further information will be forthcoming, as positive IDs have been made, and next of kin have been notified."

CHAPTER 53

SHERIFF DAN OSBORNE

My worst nightmare was coming true. I knew I had been careless leaving the leg by the campfire the night I got spooked, but I had convinced myself that all was good. Now, I sit here in this cold, sterile jail cell awaiting my fate. As I look around, all I see are blank, drab brown walls with scratches where other inmates have either carved their initials or tried to make a statement with some random saying. My mind wanders, and all I can think about is that my trial is set to start soon. If I'm found guilty, I won't be able to deal with being locked away forever. To me that is a fate worse than death.

I've scored a great lawyer to plead my case, and I feel confident that he will be able to get me released on a technicality.

Certainly, the state has no damning evidence to convict me. That hillbilly giant and snotty-nosed kid couldn't possibly have turned over evidence that could convict me, although I must admit I was shocked to find my box with all my treasures missing. If anything, it would be circumstantial and would be my word against theirs. And since I am a trusted officer of the law, I'm positive I will seem much more credible. I hope I'm not living in a fantasyland and that I'm not being delusional in my way of thinking. Just in case, I need to devise a backup plan because I refuse to be locked away. I have all the time in the world as I sit day in and day out, locked away like some kind of animal. Didn't they understand who I was and how important I was to helping the children of Mount Sierra?

I have been a pillar of the community for years and have built a foundation based on trust and bravery, putting away many criminals to keep our town safe for all. During this time, I have built so-called "friendships" with people who are indebted to me. It's time to call in a couple of favors—just to be on the safe side. I was put on this Earth to do God's work, and I'll be damned if I get put away.

That would allow so many more women to abuse their children, and I can't or won't allow that to happen. They must rot in hell. And I must be the one to carry this out or die trying.

CHAPTER 54

JONATHAN

Luke and I both agreed that we, indeed, made a great team. We reminisced about our adventures leading up to the arrest and what we could have done differently. Obviously, his getting shot was at the top of that list, but, besides that, we were proud of the job we had done. We were glad that it was once again safe to walk the streets, but, most importantly, we could rest easy, knowing the poor women could finally be allowed to rest in peace and their families to grieve. The sheriff's trial was set to take place in the next couple of weeks, and we had both been called as key witnesses for the prosecution. We were both excited to tell our adventures in court and watch from the front row as he got sentenced.

The next week Luke got released from the hospital, and my Dad insisted he, Sydney and Buffy come stay at our house to convalesce. Luke still needed a little help, and I agreed it was a fantastic idea. The more time the two spent together, the better. This was the olive branch I had been hoping my Dad would extend, and Luke reluctantly accepted only because he didn't want to be any trouble. Having Luke in my house was weird, but I loved it. It allowed me to spoil him for once. The house once again felt like a home, and the black cloud that had hovered over it, sucking the good air out, had blown away and was replaced by a beautiful rainbow. New beginnings and the promise of a brighter future. My Dad was great with Luke, too, and I watched happily as my two favorite people in the world formed a friendship. They really hit it off and spent hours telling stories about their pasts and dreams for the future. I could hear roars of laughter coming from the other room as I cooked Luke's favorites. I couldn't have asked for a better ending to a very tense beginning.

I reluctantly went back to school, and all my absences were forgiven. I experienced a very strange and foreign concept to me, because, all of a sudden, I was the most popular kid in the school. Everyone wanted to be my friend and hear about my escapades. I couldn't walk down the hall without being asked for my autograph, like I was some kind of celebrity. I found this really funny because I was just me. Just Jonathan. I wasn't sure how to take all the attention at first but quickly warmed up to the idea and enjoyed being the center of attention. For once, I had something to talk about that everyone was interested in, and it helped me come out of my shell. Even the pretty girls in school would flock around me like I was someone special. I was enjoying my newfound fame and a sense of self-worth. My Mom would have been proud of my transformation.

While I spent my days in school, Luke continued to get stronger and stronger by the day. He was almost back to normal and ready to move back to the cabin. He had become a permanent fixture in our home and our lives so much that the thought of him not being around every day made us all very sad. Plans were made to meet up every day, either for dinner or a strategy session for the upcoming trial. My Dad drove him to their AA meetings and accepted Luke's offer to be his sponsor. Having this in common cemented their bond even more. Life was good, and things were peaceful and harmonious—the way I had dreamt they could be.

Another silver lining was that my Dad somehow had either out-grown his allergies or was taking pills behind my back, because the pet fur didn't bother him any longer. He, I and Luke planned a trip to the local animal shelter to look for a dog and cat of our own. As we walked by each kennel, the dogs would come to give us a sniff and friendly tail wag. I wanted them all but knew immediately when I saw a five-year-old golden retriever that had been found as a stray that it was meant to be. I promised myself I would come back to visit and spend afternoons as a volunteer, but for now I would smother my very own Canela with hugs and kisses. We scooped her up, along with a gray striped cat we named Willow. I was on cloud nine as we rode home with my face buried in Canela's fur while Willow slept curled up in my lap.

JONATHAN

The next few weeks were a whirlwind. I had decided to take up soccer again, so my off time, when I wasn't getting bored in my classes, was spent at either soccer practice or conditioning. Luke and my Dad took turns driving me to practice. I loved my time with both of them, and having them get along so well made my life near perfect. If only my Mom were here to see how my life had taken a 180 just by wandering into the forest one lonely, cold night. If my and Luke's paths hadn't crossed, I don't know where I would be right now, and, frankly, it scares me to think about it. He was my lifesaver, and it's more clear than ever to my Dad how much gratitude he owes Luke. I also managed to squeeze in a therapy session here and there with Luke's therapist. I had come so far, but to put everything out there—knowing there'd be no judgment—was refreshing. I healed more and more every day and was finally able to accept my Mom's death. I knew she was in heaven looking down on me, and I hope she was happy with how my life was turning out after my many struggles to come to terms with the curveballs thrown my way.

On a freezing cold night in December, Luke and I were honored with a parade. It was one of the highlights of the whole year. That was a bold statement on my part, since lately my life was filled with quite a few highlights: My newfound popularity, returning to soccer, Luke and my Dad becoming friends and my acceptance of my Mom's death, giving me permission to move on with my life—not to mention the arrest of the Mount Sierra killer and my new furry friends that I couldn't seem to get enough of. The list seemed to go on and on, giving me so much joy and happiness. It was like I was making up for all the many months I mourned non-stop for my Mom to return and my Dad to come to his senses. My life had been busy and rewarding as of late.

The parade was celebrated by what looked like the whole town as well as the neighboring towns. We rode on a grandiose float while everyone cheered and waved as they huddled under blankets, drinking hot chocolate or apple cider. Luke, Sydney, Canela and I looked on with so much pride in our accomplishments. Canela was magical and everything I had ever wanted in a dog. She and Sydney had become best friends and loved wrestling and chasing balls together.

As the parade ended, the whole town met in the town square, where Luke and I became honorary mayors and got keys to the city. The Mountain View High School band played "Hail to the Chief" and I couldn't wipe off the smile that was plastered on my face for anything. I didn't want the night to end. I took a moment to reflect on how far my life had come and found it nearly impossible to remember the dark place in which I had lived. I took this as a very good sign.

After all the pomp and circumstance was over, we got the honor of meeting the families of the murdered women. It was a poignant moment as each family came to introduce themselves and share stories of their loved ones. I caught a glimpse of my Dad as he looked on with pride in his eyes. He gave me a thumbs-up and blew me a kiss! There wasn't a dry eye in the place as everyone cried tears of sadness as well as joy that they could finally put their loved ones to rest. I knew for the rest of my life that I would never forget these gracious people. We were given gifts and flowers, each one just as meaningful as the last, that I would treasure forever. I took a second to glance Luke's way, and my gentle giant of a friend was openly crying and hugging everyone in sight with the biggest smile on his face. We all shared a bond that would forever tie us together and made plans to have a huge barbecue once the weather warmed up. I loved having things to look forward to.

A week after the parade, things heated up again when the trial started. I had been looking forward to justice getting served for so long, but, now that it was here, I had mixed emotions.

Having met the families last week made everything more real, and this made me more eager than ever to put the sheriff away forever, but, on the other hand, I felt a little sorry for him. This was not an emotion I was prepared to deal with, but, as I had done research in preparation for the trial, everything I read about serial killers pointed to a dismal, abusive childhood. This made me sad for him if this is truly what had warped him into the ruthless killer he was. But then, on the other hand, nothing that happened in your childhood should give you a free pass to kill others. This confused me, and I promised myself I would try to sort it out with my Dad and Luke after the first day of testimony.

The courtroom was filled to capacity with media as well as family members of the deceased. The sheriff sat in his orange jumpsuit, handcuffed, with his head bowed. Was he remorseful for the heartache he had caused, or did he feel it was his calling to kill innocent women? It was hard for me to comprehend what was going through his mind. My mind wasn't wired like that. Thank God! As my Dad, Luke and I sat in the front row, glued to every word, I happened to look over at the sheriff at the same time that he looked at me. A shiver ran down my spine as I recalled the lifeless limbs floating in the formaldehyde, but when our eyes met at first, I didn't see a killer. Was it a façade?

For a nanosecond, I saw a damaged, abused soul not knowing right from wrong. And just as I was starting to feel an inkling of sadness for a childhood lost, his eyes turned to evil. He winked at me with the most sinister smirk as he spit in my direction. I gasped and started shaking. Both my Dad and Luke simultaneously put their hands on my knees to calm me, not knowing what had spooked me to my core. I had always taken pride in my good judgment of character, but I clearly was off when it came to the sheriff. He was evil, pure and simple, and he had the ability to become a chameleon when it suited him.

As the attorneys wrapped up their opening statements, we were told by the judge that testimony would resume promptly at 9:00 a.m. the next morning. Luke and I were not scheduled to appear tomorrow, which suited me just fine, because, quite frankly, I was really scared and very nervous. Even more so now, as I was reminded of the exchange that had taken place between the sheriff and myself earlier in the day. I logically knew I wasn't in jeopardy of any physical harm, but he was playing mind games with me that were equally as damaging. We had both been prepped by the prosecutor, but I still had a feeling of dread that I couldn't seem to shake. As much as I had been looking forward to the trial taking place so that justice could be served, I was now looking just as forward to it coming to an end.

Reading my mood, Luke had a great idea to make us forget about what was going down at the courthouse. "Let's all go pick out the tallest, grandest Christmas tree and spend the night decorating it and singing Christmas carols!" Luke enthusiastically exclaimed. With all that had been going on,

Christmas had been all but forgotten, and it was now the middle of December. My Dad and I both jumped on this idea. It sounded like just the medicine the doctor would have ordered to lighten our moods. The rest of the night was a chapter out of a self-help novel. We laughed till tears ran down our faces and reminisced about Christmases past, both bad and good. To me, though, the best part of all was being together as one, big, very happy family, making new memories and building new traditions.

Morning came around way too soon and yet not soon enough. I was dreading going to court. Our tree decorating got my mind off the trial and creepy sheriff for a short time, but once Canela, Willow and I were alone in my room, I couldn't get the sheriff's sinister smirk out of my mind. I'm sure it was meant as intimidation, and, let me be the first to tell you—it worked. I was spooked. So much that, as soon as I allowed sleep to take over, I immediately fell into another nightmare. This time, I was alone in the forest with only the sheriff. He was chasing me, wielding a machete and screaming crazy talk at me. I dodged in and out of tall pine trees while the needles pierced through my skin and got stuck in my hair. I was out of breath and sweating profusely despite the freezing cold temperatures that plagued the forest. He was quick for an older guy, and, every turn I took, he followed, coming within an arm's-length. I was desperately screaming for help, but no one came. I lost my footing as I tripped over a tree root, and he was upon me with his arm raised, ready to strike. I could see the evil look in his eyes and smell his rancid cigar-tainted breath—but then, I heard a shot ring out. He fell to the ground, which allowed me to run like I had never run before.

That's when I woke up, sweat-soaked and with my heart beating out of my chest. I never found out who had come to my rescue, but I had a sneaking suspicion that it was my Mom. She always had my back. I lay still, contemplating the meaning of my dream while cuddling Canela. I came to the conclusion that I needed to watch my back because the sheriff was running scared and out to get me.

CHAPTER 56

JONATHAN

Dressed, I made my way downstairs, reveling in the fact that we were one day closer to doomsday for the sheriff. My Dad and Luke were sitting at the kitchen table, eating a huge stack of fluffy pancakes smothered with peanut butter and syrup. There was a light dusting of snow on the ground, and the smell of the outside permeated the inside air. I loved the smell of a Christmas tree. All of a sudden, I was famished and never so happy to see my "Dads." Just seeing these two, I instantly felt safe and secure. No matter how my dream had affected me, I was determined that today was going to be a good day, after all.

The gallery of the courtroom was just as crowded as the day before, with standing room only. We took our seats in the front row, and, as the sheriff was led in, I made a promise to myself not to let him get to me again. I felt his eyes piercing through me, but I didn't give him the satisfaction of so much as a glance his way. His intimidation tactics had worked once, but I was on to his game now.

The day dragged on, with meaningless testimony from a variety of experts. The prosecution was laying the groundwork, which was important but boring to me. As much as I was scared to testify, I wanted to get it over with. The anticipation was weighing very heavily on my mind and making me anxious. I tried to daydream and lose myself in happy memories, but the tension in the courtroom was suffocating me. I had an uneasy feeling that I was getting glared at, but I resisted the urge to take a glance at the sheriff. He would have to play his mind games on someone else because I was all played out.

When the judge announced that court was adjourned for the day, I felt like standing up and doing a little dance. I needed some fresh, crisp air to clear my head and ease my soul. Just being in the same room, feet away from the sheriff, gave me the willies. We had been informed that we would be on the stand tomorrow, and knowing this, I was sure the sheriff would be after me more than usual. I thanked my lucky stars that he would once again be locked up and away from people for the night. After the evil look in his eyes yesterday, I feared what he was conjuring up in his warped, sick mind.

CHAPTER 56 ... JONATHAN

Earlier I had asked my Dad if it was alright with him if I spent the night at Luke's so we could do more prep. In all honesty, I felt a sense of security there, and I craved being around all the animals, but I didn't want to hurt my Dad's feelings. So, after we all had pizza at the local pizzeria, I stopped at my house, picked up Canela and headed over. I was so thankful my Dad understood my bond with Luke and had put his jealousy aside once and for all.

Upon entering Luke's cabin, my eyes bulged out of my head, because not only did he have the place decorated like a winter wonderland with the most spectacular tree, but he had listened to me when I had explained to him how my Mom had decorated—and it was exactly the same.

Twinkling fairy lights were hanging everywhere, and some mistletoe was hanging in the doorway. There were Christmas carols playing and a bowl of fresh popped corn was sitting next to a needle and string to make our own garland. The resemblance was uncanny, even down to the handmade clay ornaments. There were beautifully wrapped gifts in tartan-plaid greens and reds stacked perfectly under the tree. As I reached out to touch an ornament, a big, gigantic red bow caught my eye. Under it was a brand-new shiny, red Trek mountain bike!

I couldn't believe my eyes. I shrieked with excitement and jumped gleefully up and down. As I turned to thank Luke, he was standing by the roaring fire, wearing a Santa hat and the biggest smile anyone could ever have. I ran over to him, and he lifted me up into one of those bear hugs I had grown to love. I don't know how or when he had found the time to do this, but he had pulled off the best Christmas surprise, and my heart melted on the spot. "Luke, I can't ever thank you enough, not just for replicating my Mom's decorating and the bike, but, most importantly, for listening and caring enough to want to do this. It means the world to me. And you do, too," I gushed. And then we both cried. Cried for lost loved ones but mostly for the friendship and love we had found in each other.

After burning the midnight oil, I finally crashed in front of the fire, wedged between Canela and Sydney. I was anxious about being put on the stand, so I anticipated some crazy dreams, but, instead, I woke up refreshed and ready to tackle the day. I attributed this to Luke, my sleeping companions and being at the cabin. From the first time I'd walked through the door, I had fallen in love with the place, and, now more than ever, the contentment I felt could not be compared to anywhere else. Not even my rainbow room—and that was saying a lot. I immediately looked toward the far side of the room to see if I had dreamt the Christmas tree, decorations and bike—but, nope! It was all real and just as beautiful as ever.

Just as I was admiring my bike, Luke appeared out of the kitchen with a chef's hat on and an apron that looked like a Santa suit. "Good morning, son! I made you a breakfast feast to start off your day!" he said. And he wasn't kidding. There was enough food to feed a small army. He certainly took to heart the old saying that breakfast was the most important meal of the day.

Between bites of Belgian waffles and crispy bacon, we discussed the trial and what to expect. After all the research I had done on serial killers and their disregard for authority, I was concerned that things could turn ugly. I finally confided in Luke about my scary exchange with the sheriff the other day, and he assured me that *over his dead body* would he allow the sheriff to hurt me. I wasn't really worried about physical harm as much as the psychological effect he was having on me. Just another thing to add to my ever-growing list of things to address at my next shrink appointment. I had come to look forward to having a nonjudgmental sounding board.

CHAPTER 57

JONATHAN

When we arrived at the courthouse, my Dad was standing out in front waiting for us. He greeted me with a toothy smile and a hug, admitting he'd been lonely without me last night. Ever since his rehab and consistent AA meetings, he was a totally changed man. The Dad I had loved all my life was back just the way I remembered before my Mom was taken from us. And I, for one, was all onboard and overjoyed to have him back. If it weren't for the trial weighing heavily on my mind, life would be near perfect.

Since we would be testifying today, Luke and I took seats on a bench outside the courtroom, while my Dad made his way in and plopped down in the front row. I peeked in just as the bailiff was escorting the sheriff to his spot. We locked eyes. My world stopped for a moment as I watched him raise his shackled wrist to his throat. He made a movement across his throat implying that he was going to slit my throat and kill me. I gasped but stood firm. After my talk with Luke, I felt less intimidated, and I was not going to let him suck the life out of me. I shut the door and was collecting my thoughts just as the bailiff came to collect me. A quick hug from Luke, followed by a wink and a "Go give them hell, son" and I was gone. It was go time!

The air in the courtroom was filled with palpable tension. My hands were shaking as I nervously bit my nails. A bad habit I had taken up as of late. I gave my Dad a quick glance for moral support but avoided the sheriff. As I got comfortable in the witness stand, I allowed myself to look at the jury. I was glad I did because all twelve of them were staring at me with reassuring supportive looks in their eyes. This calmed my nerves a little as the questions started. Ann Bishop, the prosecuting attorney, whom I had become quite fond of, eased into the whole process, and I was allowed to tell my story from the scream on that first night to my subsequent meeting with Luke at the campfire. It was exhausting and exhilarating to tell my story step by step as it had unfolded throughout the previous months. Just as I was getting into my groove, the judge called for lunch recess.

Lunch was juicy burgers and stacks of crispy, lightly salted fries rounded off with a neapolitan shake. My Dad and Luke assured me that I had done fantastic, as we dove into our burgers. I was relieved to hear that I hadn't looked as nervous as I felt. My Dad also shared that he had taken a couple glances at the sheriff, and, every time, he had his head down. It was hard to dive into his mind to figure out what he was thinking, but I chose to think he was remorseful and defeated.

Wishful thinking, I was sure, but a boy can dream!

My testimony resumed promptly at 1:30. I was feeling comfortable and collected as the questions about the campfire resumed. The ring and fingernail I had found were entered into evidence. This evidence could be instrumental in the conviction of the sheriff, and I was a crucial part of this process. The pride I felt in myself was like no other. It gave me one of those head-swelling moments I had gotten only when playing soccer. As the day continued, I explained in detail how I started putting two and two together as I did my research. Meeting Luke, thanks to Sydney, was a stroke of pure luck, because that's when the brainstorming really began and the plans unfolded.

Surprisingly I was starting to enjoy myself while on the stand. For the first time in my life, I was making a difference, and all eyes were on me, listening intently as I explained in great detail the discovery of the dreaded box. The pictures Luke and I had taken proved to be just as important as the physical evidence. Thank God he'd used his noggin once again to think of that angle. As the pictures containing the boxes of floating lifeless limbs were shown to the jurors, I watched as horror and disgust washed across their faces. Some let out audible gasps, while others turned various shades of green and had to quickly excuse themselves to go retch. But it was unanimous that they all were appalled. The spectators reacted somewhat in the same manner, as chatter broke out in the courtroom. It was clearly getting out of control when the judge pounded his gavel so hard that the windows rattled in their frames, and I jumped a foot in the air. A ten-minute recess was called to settle things down and bring the court to order once again. The sheriff remained seated, with an evil smirk, like he was taking great pleasure in the eruption.

The afternoon session was spent in much the same way as the morning session, with question after question laying the foundation of a serial killer who had been allowed to run amok for years, using the forest as his own personal house of horrors. I found myself getting highly emotional as I relived my time with Luke in the forest. Running on pure adrenaline while being caught up in the moment had not given us time to sift through the plethora of emotions we had. It seriously ran the gamut from jubilation to immense sorrow when finding evidence. And then with Luke near death for weeks, it was a lot to compartmentalize, and I now realized I hadn't given myself time to come to terms with all that had happened. I lost it. I mean, really, really lost it. A blubbering, shaking puddle of tears, and I was humiliated.

Court was excused for the day, mainly to give me time to get my emotions in check. I thought I had come so far, but dredging up the horror that lay beneath that earth in the forest was the stuff nightmares are made of. Not only that, but I had just recently come to terms with my Mom's death. I was also reminded that I was only thirteen, when emotions ran high and out of control the majority of the time. I was once again being too hard on myself. I needed to listen to my gut, and my gut was shouting at me to take the rest of the afternoon at the cabin spending time with the animals. My Dad, thank God, was intuitive enough to see that it was most definitely not the time to question my desire to stay at Luke's again. He hugged me goodbye, told me he loved me to Pluto and back and that he would be waiting for me at the courthouse in the morning. *That* was one thing I was thankful for today.

Although the air had picked up a stiff breeze, making the temperature plummet, I bundled up and headed out, with my pockets overflowing with apples and carrots, to talk to the horses. They were always so happy to see me that it made me feel wanted. And appreciated. In all actuality it was probably my snacks that they wanted, but I liked to believe it was my company. Horses had always been given a bad rap for not being as intelligent as some other mammals, but I knew, for one, they were smart, and, more importantly, understood human emotion. Just because they weren't the best problem solvers didn't mean they didn't have the ability to learn. And feel. They had become my saving grace on more than one occasion as of late, and I was about to tap into that once again.

I returned to the cabin hours later, refreshed. Just talking to the horses, as they snuggled my neck, allowed me to get into the right headspace. I also managed to get in a ride, which further cleared the cobwebs and put things into perspective. The bottom line was, I was proud of both Luke and myself for bringing down the sheriff and allowing the families of the women to grieve. No matter what needed to be done to make the sheriff pay for the dastardly mutilations, I was going to help and deal with the aftermath later.

CHAPTER 58

JONATHAN

Snow had started falling in big billowy flakes just as I opened the door to the cabin. I was greeted by a roaring fire and the most intoxicating aroma. It was a pleasant mixture of Christmas tree and pot roast. Both Canela and Sydney jumped on me, whining in delight, like I had been gone for days. It felt good to be missed and wanted. And cared for, like Luke could only do. He had the innate ability to read my thoughts and provide me with heartfelt as well as extremely helpful advice, all while making me feel appreciated and secure. I took a moment to soak in my surroundings, and, as I did, I was overwhelmed with a sense of love and belonging. It gave me the warm, fuzzy feeling I had missed since my Mom had been taken from me.

I was brought back to reality when Luke called from the other room that I better have had worked up an appetite, because dinner was ready. As usual, the kitchen was cheery and welcoming with pots on every burner simmering some delicious concoctions he had whipped up. The fresh garden flower centerpiece on the table had been replaced with a beautiful poinsettia for the holidays. Twinkling fairy lights outlined the windows and hung from the light fixtures. He had managed to transpose the kitchen into a winter wonderland as well. Sitting down at the table, I was filled with not only gratitude but ravenous hunger.

As we dug in, he inquired about my time with the horses and if they had been as therapeutic to me today as they had been in the past. I assured him that they had once again worked their magic and that my mindset was once again on track. Talking to Luke was natural. It was like we had known each other forever, and there was never uncomfortable silence or strained conversation. It felt the way it had been between my Mom and myself, and I craved that in my life. As much as I hated what had happened to those poor women at the hands of the sheriff, I was thankful as well in a weird, selfish way. Without those tragedies, I would have never had the extreme pleasure of meeting and getting to know Luke. Without him, my life would not have taken the turn it had taken, so, for that, I was eternally grateful. I was more convinced than ever that everything happens for a reason.

The sandman had been busy last night, and, as I rubbed the sleep from my eyes, I had a clear focus on the day ahead. My sleep had once again been filled with dreams but, I was glad to say, no nightmares. My Mom had come to visit me in my dream just to tell me how proud of me she was as well as assure me that I was doing the right thing testifying. I woke up missing her more than ever. I didn't have doubts that I was doing the right thing, but at the same time, it was difficult to relive the nightmare. Especially with the sheriff sitting just feet from me glaring my way, wishing me death. I had never experienced hate like that before, and it was frightening. Nor had I ever experienced the warped mind of a serial killer. The inner thoughts he possessed were like none I could begin to comprehend—or care to, for that matter.

Snow had continued to fall throughout the night, and on arrival at the courthouse, I immediately noticed someone had built a non-traditional snowman at the top of the steps in front of the entrance. He sported a carrot nose and eyes of coal, but atop his head sat an old-time curly wig like those once worn by British members of Parliament, as well as a judge's robe. I couldn't help but marvel at people's creativity, and just the sight of it made me chuckle, which lightened my mood.

Once again Luke and I were seated outside the courtroom. Ms. Bishop, the prosecutor, promised me she would be quick and wrap my testimony up within an hour's time. I assured her I was more than prepared to do what needed to be done, but she mumbled something about not tempting fate. While I got sworn in once again, I took a quick glance at the jury. They were attentive and sitting at the edge of their chairs with bated breath. Unfortunately for them and fortunately for me, the prosecutor was true to her word, and I was excused within the hour. I breathed a sigh of relief that I had managed to get through it without a meltdown.

After a short recess, Luke was called to the stand. His stature was so large that he was squeezed in like a sardine in the witness box. He was cool and collected as he described the screams he had heard. The screams that shook him to the core and led to his investigations. He had an impressive amount of personal belongings he had collected that were entered into evidence. Each piece—from the pink ribbon to the AirPod—was attached to a name of one of the unfortunate women. Pictures of the women, smiling and full of life, flashed on the overhead. A somber calm was evident in the room as the horrendous nature of these crimes sank in. There was not a dry eye in the whole place, except the sheriff's, who sat stoic with his ever-present smirk wiped across his face.

By the day's end, Luke had finished his testimony, and the prosecution had rested their case. Tomorrow would start with the defense pleading their case and calling witnesses to the stand. The courtroom was all abuzz with talk about if the sheriff would be called to the witness stand. If he decided to, it would be a ballsy move. Legally he had no obligation to testify. Practically, even an innocent defendant may suffer serious damage on cross examination by a skilled prosecutor.

It was strongly frowned upon, especially in high-profile cases, for many reasons. When the defendant testified, it turned the case from whether the prosecution had proved its case into whether the jury believed the defendant. Typically, you want the jury to answer the first question, not the second.

We met briefly with our new friend, Ms. Bishop, and she explained what would be happening during the rest of the trial. She explained that a defendant who takes the stand has almost an impossible job, one that even most actors can't pull off. Jurors are looking for every little thing. Since the sheriff had been sitting at the counsel table, they had already had the opportunity to observe him and watch his physical demeanor. I'm almost positive they had witnessed his smirk and pompous attitude, so if the sheriff would become emotional, the jury would think they were crocodile tears. If he showed no emotion, he could be seen as cold and heartless. Plain and simple, it was a crapshoot, even if human nature says you should defend yourself at all costs. By not testifying, it would look like he was admitting guilt. It was going to be interesting to see what avenue they would take, since we all knew the sheriff was guilty as the day is long. I, personally, was looking forward to him taking the stand so I could watch him squirm. One thing was for certain: Pinocchio would have nothing on him with all the lies he surely would concoct in hopes of saving his measly soul.

CHAPTER 59

JONATHAN

I spent the night at home, mostly so my Dad wouldn't feel left out, even though my heart was at Luke's. Ever since my Mom had died, our house was a cold shell of its former self. No matter what was done to try to make it cheery, it remained sad. Too many memories remained within these walls, and my Dad and I made an agreement that, after all the trial stuff was behind us, we would put the house up for sale and buy something smaller, where we could make our own memories. Although leaving my rainbow room would be sad, I was looking forward to a change for the better.

The next morning was unseasonably warm, by Pacific Northwest standards. When we got to the courthouse, the judicial snowman was half melted and the robe sat pooled on the ground, while the wig remained askew on top of his head. Someone had posted a sign that read "Justice for the Snowman." I found this humorous and always loved to start my day with a laugh. Little did I know this would be the only thing humorous to come out of my day.

Just as my Dad, Luke and I seated ourselves in the front row, court was called to order. The morning consisted of forensic experts trying to poke holes in what I saw as a rock-solid, slam-dunk case. The members of the jury, to my dismay, were listening intently and hanging on every word. As the day continued, I started to doubt the process. I had been 100% positive there would be a conviction based on the evidence in conjunction with my and Luke's testimony, not to mention the experts, but as I sat glued to my seat, I didn't feel good at all about what I was hearing. Or seeing. The cross examination of the witnesses did very little to discredit them, and I was hitting a new low when lunch recess was called.

There was a quick meeting with Ms. Bishop, in which she assured us things were not nearly as bad as they seemed and to keep the faith. I guess you could call it a pep talk, but it did little to pep me up or ease my mind. Luke, my Dad and I were all feeling a little down in the dumps but made a pact that we would keep a positive attitude and let the process work its magic. On a positive note, being in court reaffirmed the idea of me wanting to be a lawyer and follow in my Dad's footsteps. I was in awe of my surroundings. The look of the courtroom, even the way it smelled like leather and books, made me want more. And, as always, I was reminded of my Mom. One of my favorite childhood memories with her was going to the library, where we would wander the aisles, picking out books. The smell of books was yet another memory that would always and forever conjure warm, fuzzy thoughts of her, and, for that, I was grateful beyond words.

The afternoon court session came and went. It was filled with lies upon lies. And then more lies. Character witnesses had filled the witness stand—one after another, trying their hardest to persuade the jurors in believing the sheriff was a pillar of the community. Fellow deputy sheriffs swore by his work ethic, while neighbors, past and present, told tales of him being the perfect neighbor. From maintaining an immaculate yard and always willing to lend a hand when needed—from their perspective, it was nearly impossible to believe the right man was behind bars. The sheriff sat beaming with pride, and all I could do was just hope and pray that the jurors had not been buffaloed by this latest last-ditch effort to put the sheriff on a pedestal.

Reading my thoughts, as usual, Luke made the best suggestion that we all meet at his house for dinner. He made an excuse to my Dad that he wanted him to see his place decorated for Christmas, but I could see through what he was up to. He knew I wanted and needed to be at the cabin around the animals but felt an obligation to my Dad. By bribing my Dad with sparkling cider and a friendly game of five-card stud, he convinced him, knowing I would crash by the fire, snuggling with the dogs and getting to spend the night. Luke was a fast thinker and a sly devil. He looked my way and winked happily that his plan had worked. And I must confess, I was happy, too.

It was a spectacular night, filled with good food and even better company. We had agreed the second we walked through the door that there would not be one moment of sheriff or trial talk.

We had all sat through more than our fair share of lies, from which we needed time away to enjoy ourselves and look to the future. My Dad had just told Luke about our plans to move when Luke came up with the most fantastic idea. "You must know by now how much I enjoy your company," Luke said to my Dad and me, "so why don't you build your own cabin on some of my land? I have more than enough, and nothing would make me happier than to share it with my two favorite people!" I could hear the excitement in Luke's voice and see the twinkle in his eyes. He was serious and wasn't going to take "No" for an answer. I honestly couldn't contain my excitement either. I would have the best of both worlds. Now I just needed to convince my Dad.

CHAPTER 60

JONATHAN

As the sun rose over the mountains, there was not a cloud in sight. The snow had completely melted, and my first thought was for the poor snowman. Knowing how invested people had become in his livelihood, I wouldn't be surprised to see a wake, offering up snow cones in his memory once we got to the courthouse! But what we did see was Ms. Bishop, standing at the top of the steps, waving at us to come to her. Upon seeing this, my initial reaction was one of puzzlement, immediately followed by doom. Had something bad happened? Luke placed his huge hand on my shoulder to ground me and whispered in my ear to take a deep breath and not overreact until we had details.

She explained that today would be the end of the witnesses and that closing arguments would follow before the jury deliberated. At the end of court yesterday, her co-counsel had overheard the public defender arguing with the sheriff, practically begging him not to take the stand, but the sheriff was adamant that he tell his side of the story. She wanted us to know that Luke and I would most likely be under attack and put in a bad light. No emotion should be on display from either one of us, as we potentially could be ripped to shreds and called liars and fabricators of evidence. Expect the worst, and then you won't be caught off guard, she explained. We thanked her for her heads-up and headed away from everyone for another quick pow-wow. Both my Dad and Luke knew how sensitive I was and that being verbally attacked would elicit all kinds of emotions from me. The best piece of advice they gave me was to have a thick skin and let it roll right off. We knew the truth, and that's all that mattered.

As we entered the courtroom, word must have leaked that the sheriff would be taking the stand, because it was pure pandemonium. People were pushing each other out of the way, jockeying to find a place to stand, and verbal altercations could be heard. It was apparent people were on edge, but this was ridiculous. Luckily, we had our permanent seats saved in the front row. As we settled in, I was aghast at what was unfolding in front of my eyes—in a court of law, no less! By the time the bailiff brought the sheriff in, people were standing three deep against every surface imaginable. The crowd had lulled to a low rumble, which ceased immediately as soon as the judge sat down and pounded his gavel loud enough to wake the dead. He wasn't standing for any chaos in his courtroom and proceeded to lecture on decency and love for thy neighbor. It got as quiet as a church mouse after that, and the court session was called to order.

To my dismay, the sheriff was called to the witness stand first up. As he was sworn in, I got nauseous and felt light-headed. I was immediately comforted by a hand from each of my Dads on my knees. Time to ground myself and go to my happy place while still saying present was going to take some finagling on my part, but I was convinced I was up for the challenge. I wasn't about to let anyone down, myself included. Looking around, I observed family members of the slain women I had been privileged enough to meet, mixed in with a lot of curious citizens along with press from all over the country. It was big news, and everyone was interested to see what the outcome would look like.

The sheriff sat there with a smug, condescending look—like he was something special. He was dressed in a conserva-tive wrinkled black suit, which looked to have been purchased during JFK's presidency, a skinny red tie with an American flag pin on his lapel. All defendants had the right to appear in civilian clothing instead of the standard orange prison jumpsuit to avoid the risk that the jury's judgment would be tainted and his right to presumption of innocence would be compromised. I was hoping with everything I had that I wasn't the only one who could see through his façade. I did feel assured that, while all eyes were on him, he wouldn't pull any funny business or taunt me with his mind games. This allowed me to stare long and hard at him. He had a couple days' growth of stubble but otherwise looked clean. There was a noticeable twitch in the corner of his right steely brown eye, and a layer of sweat had begun to form on his upper lip. His hands were sans shackles, and he was nervously picking at his left thumbnail. All of these mannerisms pointed in one direction—that he was running scared and a nervous wreck in preparation of what was about to go down. I, for one, couldn't have been happier.

Sitting at the edge of his chair, he brought a glass of water, with trembling hands, to his lips. He looked anything but comfortable or in control. If his body language was any indicator at all, it would shout *Guilty*! He tried to set the glass down quietly but missed the ledge. It crashed to the tile floor, spilling water and shattering glass everywhere. He cussed quietly under his breath as an audible sigh escaped his lips; all the while, I was laughing inside.

After everything was cleaned up, the judge instructed the public defender to proceed. He looked nervous and anything but confident. This led to my next question, and I couldn't help but wonder why, when one's life is at stake, you wouldn't cough up some dough for an attorney with a proven track record. I watched as he leaned over, grabbed some papers off the desk, cleared his throat and at the same time adjusted his tie. Just as I was thinking he was trying to buy time and prolong the inevitable, he tried to speak. His lips moved soundlessly—no words came out. I had been hoping the sheriff wouldn't take the stand, but, now that he had, I was mesmerized. So many questions left unanswered, but the most pressing one was . . . *Why?* What made you take so many lives?

The courtroom was so quiet that you could hear a pin drop, as everyone collectively held their breath. Sounds like the heater running, birds chirping happily in the sunshine and a pen being tapped slowly but methodically on the desk were all discernible. I looked around the room, and every single person was staring straight ahead, focused on the sheriff. The jurors had pen and paper in hand, waiting to take notes as they eagerly anticipated his testimony. A lot was riding on their verdict, and it was clearly visible that they were taking this task seriously.

Finally, halfway collecting himself, the public defender spoke, introducing himself as Jack Rigsby. Before he started his line of questioning, he continued to fumble around with his papers and collect a pen he had dropped on the floor. I couldn't help but think it was all part of his plan. Nobody could be that ill prepared, could they? Was he buying time? Ann had said that her co-counsel had heard him and the sheriff arguing about testifying. Was he second-guessing the decision? Time stood still, or so it seemed, because, when I glanced up at the clock, it read 9:12. Court had been called into session promptly at 9:00, so I was just imagining things again. I was good at that. My favorite as of late was imagining the sheriff being executed. He deserved to die at the hands of another, just as he had done to twelve women—that we were aware of. Could there be more, somewhere out there in another town or country?

Questions started off slowly, basically addressing a lot of what everyone already knew. I had a feeling these questions were to get them both comfortable and also to put the sheriff in the best light possible. I was feeling fidgety, and, as I looked around, it was apparent I was not alone. Stifling a yawn, I was just about to nod off when the judge called lunch recess, just in the nick of time. After recess, the spectators filed in, in a lot-more-civilized manner. It was good to see that the judge's speech had sunk in, and he wasn't just rambling to hear himself talk. As the sheriff was resworn in before questioning started, I noticed a bulge in his front right pant pocket. Was it the angle, or was he hiding something? Add this to the list of things that make you go *Hmmm* and cause me more concern—as if I needed anything else on the list! As it was, I would be spending so much time with my therapist that she might as well take up residency in our spare bedroom. I leaned over to ask my Dad if he noticed anything unusual but was immediately glared at by the judge, followed by a *shhhh* from my Dad. So, instead, I stewed over the possibilities of what it could be, while biting my nails to the nub.

CHAPTER 61

JONATHAN

Mr. Rigsby started off with intense questions right from the get-go, and it was apparent *go time* had arrived, and the nitty-gritty would finally come out.

Mr. Rigsby: "Sheriff, could you please explain, in detail, why you were in the forest the night you were arrested?"

Sheriff Osborne: "I am, as everyone in here knows, the sheriff, and I patrol from time to time just to make sure there isn't any funny business going on. I was having trouble sleeping that night, so I decided to wander through. After all, it is in my jurisdiction, and it is a free country."

Mr. Rigsby: "On the night in question, what made you dig up the steel red box?"

Sheriff Osborne: "To be honest, I had no idea there was a box buried. At first, I had a gut feeling that something was out of sorts. I had been in the forest numerous times throughout the years and was very familiar with the layout. On that particular night, I noticed a slight mound of dirt located under a tree that looked recently disturbed. It prompted me to investigate further."

I was appalled that he could swear on the Bible to tell the truth, and, now, here he was, telling lies. His left eye still had the telltale twitch, but, otherwise, he seemed calm and collected. I could tell by the way Luke took a breath that he was upset by this as well. The jurors were all busily scribbling notes as he spoke.

Mr. Rigsby: "What did you find in the box once you opened it?"

Sheriff Osborne: "It was empty. I stood for a moment, perplexed as to why anyone would take the time to bury an empty box. I wasn't allowed a lot of time to think about it, because all hell broke loose, and that hillbilly giant attacked me. For no reason."

Mr. Rigsby: "You are aware that twelve boxes with preserved severed limbs, as well as a decaying severed leg, were said to have been recovered from the box. What are your thoughts on that?"

Sheriff Osborne: "I can't in my wildest dreams imagine what kind of warped soul would do such a thing, let alone keep them like they were some kind of trophies to be admired later. It is appalling, and I need to be set free so I can do my job and find whoever is responsible. Justice must be served, and I promise as your elected official, it will be, or I will die trying." *Holy geez, he was laying it on thick now.* "Elected official"—like he was some kind of celebrity or someone important! How *dare* he call Luke a *hillbilly giant*? That was just rude, to resort to name-calling. Luke shifted uneasily in his chair, and I witnessed a noticeable spasm in the right corner of his mouth. I had never seen Luke lose his cool, but he was clearly affected by this. It was my turn to put my hand on his knee to calm him. He grinned and gave me a pat back.

Mr. Rigsby: "In earlier testimony, a cigar with your DNA was entered into evidence. How do you explain this?"

Sheriff Osborne: "That's simple. It was mine. I have a nasty habit of smoking cigars and an even nastier habit of not disposing of them properly. I often smoke them when I'm in the forest and throw them on the ground. It's not like litter or anything. It will act as mulch."

Mr. Rigsby: "You've been accused by the prosecution of using your position as Sheriff of Mount Sierra to your advantage, covering up the killings and not investigating them properly. Is this true?"

Sheriff Osborne: "Of course not, and it's an insult to even suggest such a thing. I take my job very seriously and have always done my best to uphold the law and make our quaint, beautiful town a safe environment for raising a family. I take offense to this, and I might have to investigate a civil suit against them when this is all said and done."

I could hardly wait till Ms. Bishop got the opportunity to cross-examine. If I didn't know the truth, I might actually believe his lies. After all, he was pretty darn convincing and a trusted man of the law. I certainly hope she had something up her sleeve, or I could foresee him getting off scot-free. The prosecution had the burden of proving every element of a crime beyond a reasonable doubt, but, right now, I was starting to doubt the process.

As the afternoon session continued, it was just more of the same: Mr. Rigsby setting up the sheriff with pre-discussed questions and answers to put him in a good light and add doubt in the jurors' minds. If I were an outsider looking in, without knowing the truth, I could see the sheriff sitting on a throne and being unjustly accused. It would soon be Ms. Bishop's job to put cracks in his lies and topple that throne, one leg at a time.

Court was adjourned for the day, and none of us felt too good about what had gone down throughout the day. We all decided that a good night's sleep was in order; hopefully, tomorrow would be the turning point we so desperately needed. I came home with my Dad, as Luke went to the cabin alone. I felt like I had deserted him, but, honestly, I was in a foul mood and only wanted to be with Canela and Willow. My Dad and I were both lost in thought, so the ride home was silent. I had zero appetite and excused myself to my room, without dinner, to think. And snuggle. There's no better medicine than the love of a dog. I could be gone five minutes to take the trash out, and, still, the dog's squeals of joy upon seeing me were heartwarming.

I spent the evening researching court cases that were on point as well as reasonable doubt. I had all the faith in the world Ms. Bishop would get the truth out, but was that going to be enough? I needed all the stars to be aligned and everyone's toes and fingers crossed with rabbit's feet in their pockets to wipe the pompous, smug look off the sheriff's face once and for all. I finally called it a night at midnight but tossed and turned before finally falling asleep, only to have a nightmare. This time, I was in court. I was me, just Jonathan, but I had morphed into an older version of myself, and, weirder yet, I was the attorney. Everyone else was exactly the same; only I had changed. I was taking Ms. Bishop's place as the prosecutor, and the sheriff was on the stand. He still had on his outdated, wrinkly suit and power tie, but the pompous smirk had disappeared. He was sweating bullets, making his white shirt have a ring around the collar. He now had twitches in both eyes and had acquired a stutter when answering my questions. I had him right where I wanted him, when he jumped up and pulled a Ruger out of his front right pocket. He started waving it in the air, yelling incoherently about doing it for the children. Then a shot rang out. Time stopped as I looked around to see if anyone had been shot. The gallery faces staring back at me had panic written all over them, but everyone seemed intact. Just as I turned to face the sheriff again, he pointed the gun at me and laughed like a crazed maniac. I tried to move but stood frozen like a statue. As I opened my mouth, nothing came out but a gasp of air. I watched in horror as my life flashed before me. Then, out of nowhere, he turned the gun on himself and shot himself in his open mouth. He slumped over immediately, leaving brain and blood splattered against the white wall. I woke up panicked, not even knowing where I was. I must have screamed because my Dad ran into my room looking like I felt and held me tight.

Thank God it was only a dream, but it got me thinking about the bulge in the sheriff's pocket yesterday.

CHAPTER 62

JONATHAN

I had mixed emotions about the start of a new day. The sun was out, trying its hardest to thaw the frozen, frigid ground but failing miserably. Although it felt wonderful to warm my face as I gazed up to the sky, it did little to warm my soul. I was out of sorts, since my nightmare had so rudely woken me up in a total panic. Not even Canela snuggles seemed to help. What did bring a smile to my face was seeing Luke standing at the top of the stairs at the courthouse entrance. He was wearing a Santa hat, and, as I got closer, I could see he was holding a present in his right hand. He handed it to me along with a huge hug. "I thought you might need these today. A little touch of home always does the trick when I'm down and out," he said. I didn't even need to open the package to know what was inside. It was warm, and the smell of vanilla and cinnamon wafted through the paper. Inside were my favorite sugar cookies that my Mom always made me. As I bit into one, it tasted divine. I immediately started to feel better, not just from the cookie but because Luke once again had put my needs first. He knew the way to my soul, and I thanked my lucky stars for the millionth time that he was in my life.

In a quick impromptu meeting with Ms. Bishop, she explained that the end was in sight. She would get her chance to question the sheriff to clarify details, and then it was closing arguments before the jury was set free to render a verdict. I voiced my concerns, and she assured me to keep the faith, that not all was lost and it wasn't nearly as bad as it might seem. All things I needed to hear and, more importantly, wanted to believe in, but I couldn't shake the feeling that this was not going to end well. My gut instinct very rarely failed me, and my gut was speaking to me loud and clear.

The courtroom was filling up to maximum capacity once again. Everyone looked tense, and there was little joking—or smiling, for that matter. This comforted me in an odd way, knowing I was not alone with my feelings of doom.

As the sheriff was escorted to the stand and resworn in, I took a long, hard look at him. His stubble was more dense, his hair wasn't as neatly combed as it had been in the past days, and his suit looked as if he had slept in it. All in all, he looked like an unmade bed. One that had been tossed and turned in. Looking at his pocket, I reaffirmed what I had noticed yesterday. There was definitely a bulge, but I couldn't make out the outline.

Obviously guns were forbidden in the courtroom, but he was the sheriff, after all, with many connections on the inside. After my dream, I was more convinced than ever that he was packing heat. I was also more convinced than ever that no good would come out of it.

Mr. Rigsby had pretty much covered everything in the previous day, so all he did was regurgitate the lies. Much to my dismay, the sheriff's overall appearance added to the whole *woe is me* persona: an innocent man, wrongly accused and stripped of his official duties, all while being locked in a cell like a caged wild animal. It all made sense to me now. He looked like a homeless person for a reason. It was all part of his plan to get the jurors to feel sorry for him. Man, he was devious, and I prayed that they weren't that easily influenced and wouldn't fall for it. Talk about grasping for straws!

As we got back from the morning recess, it was finally Ms. Bishop's turn to reverse the damage. The more she reiterated what had been said, the more agitated the sheriff became. He yelled that he had already explained what happened in great depth, and he took offense to her hounding an innocent man. Cracks started showing in his façade. Was it her plan to wear him down until he totally lost it? If it was, it was starting to work. One question after another, he held firm on his story, but the telltale twitch was still ever-present. He wasn't nearly as cool and collected as he was trying to appear. And I, for one, was here for it.

It was fascinating to watch Ms. Bishop in action. I sat riveted in my seat, waiting to hear the final question that would topple his throne and crumble him into a million pieces of useless flesh. The more she asked, the less composure he showed. He was playing the blame game now and accusing Luke and me of setting him up and not only planting evidence but fabricating it. He went so far as to blame Luke and me as the ruthless killers and using him as our patsy. When Ann reminded him that his DNA had been found on all the evidence, the only lame answer he could come up with was that we had transferred his prints onto everything after we had broken into his office and stolen a print off his desk. It was ludicrous and absolutely baseless. I looked at the jury, and I could see a couple of them shaking their heads in dismay. He was losing them, and I could feel it as much as he could. The nail in the coffin that sealed the deal was *How could he explain his dried blood on the towel that housed the severed leg?*

You see, the night Luke and I opened the box to that gruesome display, everything had been turned over to the authorities to run tests on. What we didn't know at the time was that, somehow, the sheriff must have cut himself, and his dried blood was found alongside the blood of Alexa Hopkins on the towel. He sat dumbfounded, at a loss for words. It was apparent that this damning evidence was news to him. As he opened his mouth to speak, spittle ran down his chin. His eyes bulged in his head, and he jumped up, knocking over the microphone. This prompted the judge to pound his gavel repeatedly while screaming *"Order in the court!"* Some of the spectators were out of their seats, running for the door, while others sat frozen, unable to move. Either that or unwilling to, for fear of missing out of the biggest scoop this area had ever seen. There was pandemonium everywhere you looked.

The judge was trying desperately to get control of the bedlam. This was just the distraction the sheriff had hoped to accomplish. In one fell swoop, he jumped over the witness stand, and, for some crazy reason, started yelling, *"Save the children!"* What happened next wasn't totally unexpected by me. He fired a shot in the air. This caused more disorder, as the spectators were running for the door, pushing people out of their way and trampling others. I hadn't even realized that my Dad and Luke had both jumped up and formed a shield around me. The only good that was coming out of this disaster was that it seemed like a slam dunk for a conviction.

Ten minutes later, some normalcy had returned to the courtroom, and it had quieted to a low roar. The people who were left were on edge and looked spooked beyond words. As court was called to order, the sheriff was nowhere to be found. He had disappeared into thin air during the mayhem. It seemed pretty fishy to me that nobody had seen him leave, but it only affirmed what I had suspected all along: He had the majority of the sheriff's department in his back pocket, ready to help in a flash. The judge was rattled but remained stoic while instructing everyone to go home for the day and return tomorrow morning as usual.

CHAPTER 63

JONATHAN

Once again, I went home with my Dad and begged off on dinner. I was exhausted. The past months had started to take their toll on me, and I was really looking forward to having chill time, hopefully in the very near future. As I snuggled in my bed with Canela and Willow, I kept hearing noises outside my bedroom window. If I didn't know any better, I could swear someone was throwing pebbles at my window. *Ting. Ting. Ting.* I tried to ignore them, but curiosity got the best of me. As I peeked between my blinds to my left, I saw nothing, but as soon as I turned to the right, my eyes couldn't believe what I was seeing. My breath caught, and I think I screamed, but I couldn't be sure.

There was a spotlight facing an old oak tree in our side yard. Attached to a big, thick limb was a noose with a body hanging limply from it. I immediately bolted out of bed and flew down the stairs, yelling for my Dad. Poor guy had been quietly reading in front of the fire when I scared the bejeebers out of him. Running through the front door, Canela and my Dad at my heels, I stood dumbfounded as I stared straight at the sheriff, hanging lifeless in front of me. Out of the corner of my eye, I saw a flash of a person running from the scene. I assumed it was his accomplice, but I wasn't sure of anything at this point. My mind was racing as I stood in disbelief. There appeared to be something pinned to the sheriff's jacket, but I wasn't in any state to go one step closer to him than I already was. My Dad approached him slowly and cautiously, as if he was going to come to life and be on the attack, as I ran in the house to call Luke and 911, not necessarily in that order. Not surprisingly, Luke showed up first. He was as much in a state of shock as we were. We all wanted to see justice served, but I never would wish death on anyone. I couldn't help thinking that we were partially responsible for this, and it gave me shivers. Ultimately the sheriff had only himself to blame for his actions, but it still got me thinking about why he would go to such great lengths—and why here? I was sure it had been well thought out, just like the forest had been for his killing spree. Unfortunately, his reasons died with him, and we would never know what made this lunatic tick. I was more than confident we were better off not knowing.

We saw lights and heard sirens in the distance and knew our time was limited. Once they arrived, all hell would break loose. Just then, my Dad walked in with what had been pinned on the sheriff. It was a note addressed to "L & J." With shaking hands, Luke began to read it out loud.

To the Hillbilly Giant and Snotty-Nosed Kid:

I hope you're happy. This is all your fault because you stuck your nose in where it didn't belong. Since it doesn't matter anymore, I will admit my guilt, but not for the reasons you think. I was saving the children of Mount Sierra from years of neglect and abuse at the hands of their neglectful, mean, heartless mothers, just like mine had been. Now you will have their fate in your hands. The pleasure I derived by killing those horrible women gave me a thrill like no other.

Being locked away for the rest of my life, not being able to save more children, is a fate worse than death, so I have chosen the latter. I have solicited help from true friends to help with this journey, but don't waste your time trying to figure out who. We learned our lesson and covered our tracks better this time. What's life without a lesson learned?

Sincerely,
Your Worst Nightmare

(P.S. One more little fact that will keep you up at nights . . . Mount Sierra has not been the only place I've lived. Food for thought, you two losers!! I look forward to my afterlife so I can taunt those abusive mothers from my grave!!!)

OMG! Was he crazy? In my research, I had read numerous psychological studies that described serial killers as being raised by abusive mothers. This clearly sounded like the case here. How bad had his childhood been for him to turn into this kind of psychotic, deranged maniac? Luke spoke first and brought me out my grim thoughts to the present. "Well, that explains a little bit. I think we're all better off not knowing any more. I'm afraid this kind of stuff is what nightmares are made of," he said. My Dad and I were in full agreement that a truer statement had never been made.

The rest of the night was a blur. More officers than I could have imagined were deployed and swarming our property. Neighbors awakened by the sirens and lights were busily peeking through blinds, trying not to look conspicuous—but failing. We called Ann so she could be in the know. There was no point in us showing up for court tomorrow. In an odd way, I was going to miss it. I was looking forward to the sheriff being sentenced to life behind bars without parole. He had taken the cowardly way out, but nothing he had done shocked me at this point in time. After hours of questioning and the coroner taking the body away, we were finally left in peace. We were emotionally drained. So many questions still left unanswered. Did the sheriff imply that he had been on a killing spree prior to taking up residence here? The thought of that was too daunting to consider, but there was always tomorrow.

EPILOGUE

The next few months were a whirlwind. We had all started to heal. Slowly but surely.

Luke and I learned what gratitude was all about. The grieving families were so genuinely thankful and praised us to no end. We had done good, Luke and I. We were an unbeatable team, and I had a sneaking suspicion that we would get the urge to tackle some other crimes along the way. Knowing us both, it would most likely be sooner rather than later, but, for right now, we were content with settling into our new role as hometown heroes.

Christmas has come and gone. It was magical in every way. My new Trek bike from Luke was definitely a highlight and very much loved and appreciated, but the real highlight of the season was all the new traditions we had started. Just me and my two Dads building memories and creating a future that looked nothing but bright. Life was good. Better than good. It was fantastic for me and Canela in every way. Cloud nine and I had recently gotten reacquainted, and it felt wonderful.

I'm pleased to report Luke is as good as new and that his friendship with my Dad is flourishing. They really are two peas in a pod, with the same interests, whether it be sports or movies and everything in between. But, most important, is the unconditional love they both have for me. I have decided to keep Luke's letter with the confession to myself, because, truthfully, it is a moot point. I see no reason to dredge up something that can't be changed. What is the old saying? *Let sleeping dogs lie.*

My Dad has made a complete 180 and is happier than I have seen him since my Mom passed. He is volunteering at a suicide hotline and brushing up on the law so he can retake the bar. We have started construction on our new house on an acre of Luke's land. Luke is ecstatic about the idea, and I must admit that I am, too. My Dad has promised me that I can have as many animals as I want. This is one promise that I am bound and determined to see into fruition. I am counting down the days!!

On a personal note, I am thriving at school and enjoying it for the first time ever. Taking up soccer again has been a godsend, and I am pleased to report that my bionic leg hasn't rusted without use. The craziest thing of all is that I have friends again. I finally feel like I fit in and have my eye on a girl in my class. There is a St. Patty's Day dance coming up, and I am hoping that she will ask me to be her date. What's ironic about her is that she has the same name as my Mom . . . Emma. Somehow, I don't find this a coincidence and know in my heart my Mom had a hand in it. My nightmares are gone, and I am happy to report that my dreams are filled with happy memories and visits from my Mom. I know she is smiling from heaven, and that makes me happy. But knowing how proud she will be of the man I am becoming, even if it has taken me 12,982 hours to get here, makes me the happiest of all.

ABOUT THE AUTHOR

Donna Scuvotti is retired and lives in the Bay Area with her husband, three dogs and a cat. When not writing, she loves spending time with her family and taking her lab, golden retriever and weimaraner on long walks or to the local dog park. She loves to travel with her husband and looks forward to many adventures in the near future.

Thank you for reading *Just Jonathan*! If you'd like to be notified about upcoming releases, sales and other promotions, join Donna Scuvotti's mailing list at . . .

info@donnascuvottiauthor.com

(Your info will never be shared.)

Enjoy the first chapter from her next adventure with Jonathan in *Justice for Jonathan* due out spring 2022.

Sundays are my favorite day of the week. I had never really given it much thought until recently, when it just hit me. It's genius, really, like a do-over if the past week was crap. I've been having a lot of those, lately—crap weeks, that is.

Mainly because I can't seem to focus. I keep finding myself daydreaming. Living in the past when I was a lost soul, just thirteen years old, suffering and trying to come to terms with the loss of my beloved mom. The year was 2019, which seems like a lifetime ago, but in all actuality, it was only two decades ago. How is it possible that twenty years has gone by, just like that?

I guess it's true what they say, whoever "they" is. I have yet to figure that out. Time really does fly the older you get. I haven't met a person who can tell me otherwise. The time between birthdays or Christmases as a child felt like eternity. Now it happens in the blink of an eye. I can only imagine how scary this will be as I age—hopefully gracefully. But all the same, I just want to age. I want to look back at my life with awe and excitement and be able to tell my grandchildren about my escapades as I traveled the world.

Not everyone is granted this, and that's why I feel so strongly about it. My poor mom, whom I still miss desperately, wasn't. She was taken from me by a drunk driver when she was just thirty-nine. Not many things anger me as much as people who take life for granted. My motto has always been to get the most out of each day. Living clean, loving hard, and respecting others is how

I live my life. Such a tragedy that day was. Looking back, I can see how that day molded me into the man I am today. I often wonder how my life would be different if only I could turn back time.

Just as I was making my way down that dreaded rabbit hole, I was startled out of my funk with a loud, urgent bang on my door.

My first impulse was to pretend like I was out for the afternoon. But my melancholy mood would not benefit anyone, least of all me, so I responded.

"Come in," I said half-heartedly. "The door's open."

Brie, my personal secretary/paralegal, stumbled in looking like she'd been caught in a cat fight. And lost. Her usual coiffed appearance was nowhere in sight. Her blonde hair was in a top-knot that was half falling out, her makeup was smeared, and her pale blue blouse was missing a couple of buttons—next to a massive red spot that looked like fresh blood. Needless to say, she was frantic when she spoke.

Barely audible, she managed to utter, "Mr. Elliott, I . . . um . . . I—" before her mouth became a grimace. A puff of air escaped as she tried once again to speak. Then she collapsed on the floor next to my desk.

I ran to her side, knocking over my chair as depositions went flying here and there. I'm pretty sure I yelled at the top of my lungs for help, because within a matter of seconds my office was filled with fellow attorneys and other staff members.

All hell broke loose, and the next hour or so was a bit of a blur as chaos ensued. Through all the noise I heard someone call 911. As we waited, I bent to check for a pulse.

Her once-beautiful blue eyes were rolled back in her head and a mixture of spit bubbles tainted with blood formed around her lips. Her pulse was weak and slow, and her breathing was shallow.

I knew from years of watching medical dramas on TV she was in a bad way. In such a bad way that I was afraid I would be witness to her last breath, and this terrified me. Death was not something I ever cared to witness again after watching my mom take her last breath.

It still haunted me.

In desperation I could see Brie was trying to talk as I begged her to please hold on, that help was on the way.

I lowered myself next to her and put her manicured hand in mine. I couldn't help but notice her hand had fresh scratches and a bruise was already beginning to form. Two of her nails were broken, and all that was left were jagged, sharp edges. As I put my ear next to her mouth, I could smell a trace of her Jo Malone perfume, which I'd grown accustomed to.

Brie let out the shallowest of breaths and whispered what sounded like "phew bloop," but it made no sense. Just as I was trying to get her to repeat herself, the paramedics burst through the door—at the same time she took her last breath.

If you enjoyed this book, please consider leaving a review on Amazon or Goodreads, or simply telling your friends. Reviews and word-of-mouth recommendations are the best way to help readers find great new reads, and to support independently published books and the authors who write them.

Follow her at . . .

www.donnascuvottiauthor.com

Made in the USA
Las Vegas, NV
14 October 2021